CHARLIES

W.G.GRAHAM

Acknowledgements

Moira Galbraith and Gary for the cover illustration.

Disclaimer

The characters and events in this novella are entirely a work of fiction, as is the distillery Company of MacDonald Fraser. Glenkinchie whose reputation is impeccable, is the one and only whisky distillery in East Lothian, and well worth a visit.

ISBN:978-0-9576818-4-2

Copyright@2015 W.G.Graham

CHARLIE'S GOLD

Prologue

April 1992

    He had visited old Archie in his own home and the nurse after having announced his arrival to her patient had made a discreet withdrawal, leaving him alone with the dying man, whose face he scarcely recognised so emaciated was it. The staring bulging unseeing eyes accounted for half the face; the hollow jaws sucking in the last shallow breaths. This surely could not be his friend.
    "Archie, it's me Jock," he drew up a chair by the bedside and bent closer as his old friend waved a feeble hand in acknowledgement.
    The terminally ill man drew in a deep breath and crooked a scrawny hand for Jock to draw closer.
    After a few whispered words, Jock Fraser rose and crossed the room to a large desk, opening a drawer to extract a key and use it to open the wall safe behind.
    Back home, Jock sat staring at the wall, the sheets of white paper held loosely in his hand. As if in a trance he lifted the half filled glass of whisky to his trembling lips, and sipped, letting the fiery liquid slowly trickle down his throat.
    After a few painful moments he set his glass down on the arm of his chair. This could not be true what his oldest friend had written. He had known Archie MacDonald since his schooldays, and had always regarded him as nothing other than an honest man.
    Jock sighed and stared down at the paper in his hand and tears came to the old man's eyes. The document was not Archie's last will and testament, but a confession: A confession which he had kept secret from his own son, who had sadly passed on.
    The old man lifted the whisky glass to his lips. What was he to do? Should he burn the three sheets of paper? Or had Archie's grandson, Simon, the right to know what they contained? Should

Archie's confession become public it would ruin the Company, a Company which Archie had built up since the Second World War, and had made him an equal partner.

Jock set the glass down. Yet this was a confession he could not live with. He would keep the papers, even if it was to restrain Simon MacDonald and his headstrong ways. The man gave a shudder. When his own time came the young tearaway would own the entire business, and that young man's only thought was to sell the distillery Company of MacDonald and Fraser. No, he would keep it safe meantime, and should it prove necessary, destroy it when the time came.

CHAPTER ONE

Another Monday I thought, the dismal June weather suited my mood. I unlocked the door of my office with the sign 'West Barns Private Investigator' already peeling on the glass panelling, and pushed the door open against the bumph of mail lying on the floor: brochures, charity appeals, ads for furniture and Chinese takeaways, my thoughts that it was the start of another weary week, never knowing how wrong I could be.

As I reached my desk, crammed in the corner of an already crammed tiny room, the telephone rang, and I lifted it with a sigh, it would be old Mrs MacKenzie asking if I had managed to find her dog. However, to my surprise it was my older brother Fenton, two years older and the same weight in kilos heavier than me.

"Thought I'd give you a bell wee man," he said in a pleasantly annoying voice. I was not quite ready to be cheery so early in the morning. "I have been seconded to Teuchter land for a few weeks, so I won't be able to meet you at our usual watering hole."

"You'll do anything not to stand your round, brother of mine," I answered, feigning disappointment.

"Well, it is what it is, as they say in China."

"Funny, they say that here in North Berwick as well," I answered scanning the mail on my desk, and lifting a leaflet for a plea to adopt a tiger. Bloody stupid thing I thought where had I room for a tiger, and even if I had, it probably would not be house trained, still it could have been worse, it could have been an elephant. "Have you nothing better to do with the public's money, Detective Inspector Fenton Barns?" I asked.

Fenton chuckled. "Only to give you my number and hotel up in Inverness just in case you make your way up here sometime."

"Some hope," I answered, not knowing how wrong that statement was to be.

A few minutes after my call from my beloved brother, there was a knock on the door, and an attractive face of a woman in her early-thirties peered at me through the partially opened door.

"West Barns: detective?" she asked taking a step inside.

I rose, and motioned her to come in. Should this have been an old Philip Marlow novel it would have given him an opportunity to wisecrack about her having legs up to her armpits and an hour glass figure with the sand stacked in all the right places, instead, I merely managed to say, "Please have a seat. I'm glad you called on your own," I pointed to my one and only chair. "How can I be of assistance to you?" I asked as I sat down.

My crack about the chair did not go down well, and she gave a polite smile, as she examined my chair for dust before lowering her prim figure on to it. Her smart blue suit rode up a fraction and I glimpsed slim legs to match the rest of her figure.

"I will come to the point, Mr Barns. My name is Amanda MacDonald. My husband is Simon MacDonald of MacDonald and Fraser and Company. Perhaps you have heard of us?"

I certainly had. MacDonald Fraser as it was better known, was the biggest distillers in the area, not to mention their various other outlets such as kilt makers, glassware and every other commodity connected with 'Scottishness.' But none of your trashy memorabilia that sold in some tourist towns. I swallowed and saw a cheque for next week's rent float past.

"My husband's senior partner Mr Fraser has disappeared and I...we would like you to find him for us."

I swallowed again, and asked, "How long has he been missing?"

"Since Wednesday of last week."

"Five days?" I mused. "Have you informed the police?"

The raven hair head gave a shake. "No. That is why we seek to hire you, should hire be the correct term." She sat back in her chair and began to explain. "This weekend, we shall be putting on our biggest promotion in the history of the Company, and we can well do without any adverse publicity. It would not look well if the senior partner was unable to attend because he has gone missing."

She saw my look and went on to explain. "The old..b.. Old Jock has done this sort of thing before. You see his first love has...is treasure hunting. This started a long while ago with my husband's grandfather, Archie, who founded the Company and who made old Jock a full partner after Jock came out of army at the end of the last War. Unfortunately, old Archie, passed away just over two months ago. You may have read about it?" I nodded and uttered the appropriate sounds of sympathy. "I believe Old Jock has not really got over it and perhaps this is his way of dealing with it."

She halted and I waited for her to continue. When she did not, I asked, "Why me, instead of those Edinburgh agencies? I'm sure they're more adept at this sort of thing."

"The higher you go the more likely it is to leak out, this sort of thing has a habit of doing so, so we would like to keep it as low key as possible."

"Then you've come to the right place, you don't get any lower key than me, I'm strictly double bass."

She did not see the joke, but looked me squarely in the eye. "Will you take the case, Mr Barns? If so, we can provide you with all the background and information necessary."

Not awaiting my answer, the lady rose. "Shall we say, seven this evening?" She opened her handbag and handed me a business card. "All the information is on there. However, should you decide not to take the case, please be good enough to let us know." She stared at me in a way that only the powerful and rich people can do when they mean to scare you. "You will of course treat this meeting as strictly confidential."

While I glanced at the card I heard her say, "We shall double your usual fee, of course."

Now, instead of the card, all I could see was a huge bank cheque, and I nodded my acceptance. Whether I succeeded or not, I was sure of the rent for a week or so.

Old Jock Fraser's house, was an old Victorian style mansion, set in its own grounds, and I drove up the long driveway to the house where a black Porsche and a silver Mercedes were parked side by side. I patted the dashboard of my far from new Ford telling it not to feel too embarrassed by such company, and got out.

It did not take long for the front door to open, as curious eyes had watched my approach from one of the large bay windows, and I took an instant dislike to the man who stood there, though we had never met. His cold stare took me in from head to toe, and I now knew how my Ford must feel.

"Mr Barns I presume?" he said, standing back to let me enter.

"The same," I said, and followed him down the long corridor, where glassy eyed deers stared down at me from the walls. "Must have been some stag party," I chuckled.

'Cold Eyes' did not respond to my wit, and I was relieved when we came to a large well furnished lounge where sat my new client.

"Mr Barns. Glad you decided to take up our offer," Amanda

MacDonald rose as she greeted me, the nuance in her voice leaving me with no illusions as to this being nothing other than a business arrangement; not that I expected to be welcomed as one of the family, but a little friendliness would not have gone amiss.

As I stood there in the middle of the room, she introduced me to the others. "The gentleman who you have just met is my husband, Simon." From where he sat across the room, 'Cold Eyes' gave me a nod; no attempt to shake my hand; well after all I was the hired hand. She turned slightly to the remaining member in the room. "And this is our General Manager, Neil Grant."

"For the moment." Simon MacDonald gave a grunt, which the younger man appeared to ignore as he crossed the room to shake my hand.

"Pleased to make your acquaintance, Mr Barns. I do hope you can find Mr Fraser for us."

"I hope so too." I gave the man my warmest smile; as I felt I would need an ally if I was to find out really what was going on. The blurb about wanting to keep old Jock's disappearance a secret did not hold water. I was simply engaged, as this little lot did not think I would be capable of finding my way home, least of all their senior director.

"Take a seat Mr Barns," Amanda invited, and I took a seat on a settee facing the window where I could see my old car sitting forlornly in the driveway.

"Perhaps, I should tell you what has happened," Simon said. "My grandfather Archie, passed away a little over two months ago. My father died some years earlier," he explained. "Jock has been unable to get over what has happened. Perhaps that is why he is missing. To let you understand my grandfather and old Jock were friends for many years, they both had a hobby of treasure hunting, especially trying to find Prince Charlie's gold, which they believe is buried somewhere around Loch Arkaig.

My grandfather built up the business during the War whilst Jock was in the army. My grandfather was not called up because he had had an accident when mountain climbing in Germany in 1936. By the time the War was over, he had built up quite a business and in so doing made Jock a full partner."

"Old Jock still treasure hunted until old Archie's death," Amanda said, crossing to a side table. "Coffee, Mr Barns?"

I gestured no, at the same time as I saw the Mini Cooper speed up the driveway and come to an abrupt halt in a hail of flying gravel. The door opened and the figure of a young woman stepped hurriedly out of the car.

"Sue." Amanda said with a sigh, as watched the figure make her way to the front door.

Simon drew in a breath, annoyed by the interruption.

I heard the door open and close and the sound of footsteps in the hallway.

"Hello folks, any word of 'Gramps,'?" I heard her say as she entered the room.

"Not yet," Amanda replied.

The newcomer drew to a halt and gave me a look.

"This is Mr West Barns. We have engaged him to find Jock," Amanda explained.

I rose. "How do you do," I greeted her. My heart skipped a beat. The girl was in her mid twenties, a few years or so younger than myself, and was lovely, and her blue eyes stared at me hopefully, as she brushed back a strand of blond hair, and said hello.

Sue turned back to the others. "Is there still no word of Gramps?" Her voice held a note of concern.

"Not since you got that text from him last week," Neil said.

I looked at Sue. "You have heard from Mr Fraser last week?"

She nodded. "He said he had found it."

"Found what?" I furrowed my brows.

"Could not have been that damn gold he and my grandfather were always on about," Simon said angrily, taking a cup of coffee from his wife.

"If he has, it will be worth a fortune," Neil said quietly.

"Is money all you folk ever think about!"Sue stormed. "The old man could be lying dying or injured somewhere or worse." Her cheeks had turned a bright red.

"More likely to be shacked up with one of his old flames!" Simon sneered, setting down his cup on the coffee table.

Sue drew in a deep breath, and threw me a look to gauge my reaction.

"It's all right. If Mr Barns intends to search for Jock, he deserves to know about him," Amanda said. "The old man never married, but he still likes the women-even at his age." She gave me a look, asking if I understood.

"Which is why you're around Sue," Simon grunted. He saw my look, but before he could continue, clearly embarrassed, Sue explained.

"He knew my grandmother very well, and continued to keep in touch after my mother was born, which is why he offered me a job as his personal secretary."

"And that's why you need not worry should our promotion not go well." Neil said sternly. "It could be sink or swim for us, Mr Barns, should this promotion fail. Most of what we have, is invested in this project."

"Thanks to you and the Old Man," Simon said angrily, sitting back on the sofa.

"Well had it been left to you, the entire business would be up for sale," Neil spat out, clenching his fists by his side.

"It could well be, now that the old man's not here," Simon roared at him.

"That's enough from both of you," Amanda sharply interceded.

I had hoped the altercation would continue, so that I might learn more about this rich divided family, or should I say bunch of people, before giving a discreet cough.

"When Mr Fraser texted you," I interrupted, "Did he say where he was? Or when he was likely to return?" I asked the girl.

"No. Only that he had found it and would be back for the promotion."

"Did he leave anything in his office or at home that might give a clue as to his whereabouts?"

"He has a wall safe in his office at the rear of the house," Neil offered.

"Could there be something in it that would help as to find out where he is?"

"If there is, he is the only one that has a key. He carries it with him at all times. He has a spare of course, but God only knows where that is. Not even his solicitor has one. Silly old bugger," Simon said bitterly.

I turned back to the girl. "Could you show me the text, please?" I asked.

Sue rummaged in her bag, drew out her phone and tapped in to the appropriate message, then crossed the room to hand me the mobile.

I took it and looked at the text which was as she had said, also mentally noting the date and time. Thanking her I handed it back.

I turned to the others. "If one of you has a photo it would help?" I looked at both MacDonalds'.

"I thought you might need this." Amanda handed me a photo she had lifted from the coffee table.

I studied the picture of a silver haired old man in his late seventies. The face was tanned, the smile warm as he faced the camera.

"Do you think it likely that he is up at this.... Loch Arkaig place?" I looked at each in turn.

No one seemed to appreciate my description, until Sue ventured. "I believe that is where his last text came from."

"And his text, 'I have found it?' Could this mean the treasure he has been searching for?"

The laughter from Simon that followed my question was both loud and course. "Treasure my arse, Mr Barns. Jock was about as close to finding Charlie's gold as I am to my first dinner."

"All the same, it would be ironic, would it not Simon?" Neil said retrieving his composure. "All these years those two old friends had searched for something most folk have come to regard as nothing other than a fable. Or, if in fact there was any gold at all, it has long since been snatched up by greedy clan chiefs. And now that your grandfather is dead, old Jock wins the prize. Ironic…ironic," Neil laughed.

I knew Neil was baiting his employer, and I waited for his reaction, again waiting to hear something to my advantage, but before Simon could reply, Amanda intervened, staring at the floor as she offered her opinion. "Well, at least it gave Simon's grandfather and old Jock a purpose in life; a break from the continual pressure of the firm. And now that Archie is dead, Jock Fraser has simply seen it as a wayof coping with his grief."

"If only he had decided to go walkabout after the promotion, and not leave us with all the explaining to do about his absence: not to mention the extra work." Again the bitterness in Simon's voice gave me a reason for disliking him even more.

"What about 'Gramps'?" Sue exclaimed. She rose and walked to the window where she turned to confront the other three. "All I'm worried about is that he is all right. The bloody promotion can wait."

"Easy for you to say young Sue when it's not your Company and all it stands for that is at risk."

"There are quite a lot of people who depend upon us for their livelihood." This time it was Neil who spoke.

Sullenly Sue returned to her chair and sat down.

"Where do we go from here? Or to be precise, you, Mr Barns," Amanda's voice was soft.

"I take it you have contacted the hotel where he last stayed; hospitals etc.," I replied, letting my eyes drift from one to another.

"He usually stays at, 'The Grand' in Fort William," Amanda offered. "But we have checked that."

"I called all the hospitals including those in Edinburgh, and again when I got back from York today. No luck." Sue, gave a shrug.

I nodded and got up. "Best thing I can do is leave tomorrow for Fort William, and see what I can find out."

"Can I come along? I have been up there when Gramps took me on one of his 'hunts.' I might be of some help." Sue asked hopefully.

Had it been anyone else in the room who had asked the question, my answer would have been an instant, no, but as it was this delightful young woman who had asked, I could scarcely contain my excitement at having her for Company, especially as I was likely to be up there for at least a day or two, perhaps more, and The Grand was not exactly two star accommodation. "If it would make you feel better, why not."

"I think you should first ask my permission, Sue." Simon's eyes stared angrily at the girl. "You know we are up to our ears in work for this promotion."

I came to the girl's defence. "It would help. And it could save time in the long run, if the young lady is acquainted with the district, which I surely am not."

"Let her go, Simon," Amanda urged her husband. "You won't get much work out of her, with her mind on her Gramps all the time."

Simon gave a shrug of resignation. "All right. But only for a couple of days. And let me know what's going on."

"That's my job, Mr MacDonald," I said as politely as possible, also to ingratiate myself with this lovely girl.

Sue's face lit up, and I added as I made for the door, "Meet me at the multi-car park in Edinburgh at eleven tomorrow morning."

"Why so late Barns, are we not paying you for a full day's work? Simon rose to face me as my hand closed around the door knob.

"That you are. However, there are one or two things that I need to know before I leave for our wild Highlands. Unless you have anything to add that might be of assistance, that is, such as anything written or otherwise, that Mr Fraser might have left behind?"

When no one replied, I wished them all a good evening, with a final warning to Sue not to be late.

I had learned all I wanted to know about Prince Charles Edward Stuart, and the 1745 Jacobite Rebellion at this stage, and made my way down to the multi- storied car park where I met Sue already waiting, and together we went for my car.

"As you've done this sort of thing before, I suppose you have brought all the right gear for a little mountain climbing?" I joked.

"Naturally," she smiled at me, amused by my question.

I kept my eyes on the road as much as I dared, happy to be in the company of a girl like this.

"You really should inform the police," I suggested, giving her a sideways glance.

"You have heard why we can't." Sue gave a little sigh.

"You really think old Mr Fraser will still be up there?" I nodded at the road ahead.

"I can't think of any other place he might be. That last text said he had found it, whatever 'it' might be." Sue looked out of the window as she said it. "The poor old soul might be lying hurt somewhere. There is no need to think the treasure is anywhere near the loch itself. Indeed, it may well be near to Loch Morar, or Glen Pean or other places nearby."

"You really believe in this treasure, don't you?" I said, manoeuvring out from behind a lorry, and the way I had done it I thought the driver's vocabulary would not be as articulated as his lorry.

"The two old pals did for most of their lives, although it would be ironic if Gramps has found it, now that old Archie is dead."

"How come Gramps came to know your grandmother, Sue?"

"It's a long story," the girl sighed.

"We've got time and I have nothing better to do than listen," I urged, and tried not to sound as if it would keep me from falling asleep at the wheel.

"I don't quite know how Gramps came to meet my grandmother, but for a time old Mr MacDonald also visited her, especially during the War. My mother said she understood Gramps and my grandmother had been engaged for a time, but I really don't know if this was true or not. After my mother was born he stopped coming for a time. My grandfather died during the war, although I don't know how. After my own father died, Gramps came back."

"But you don't believe he is with your grandmother now?" I asked, accelerating.

Sue shook her head. "Granny or my mother would have told me, especially if there was anything wrong."

"So we're back to square one," I said moving back into the slow lane. "When you drove up to Fort William, did you travel in Gramps's car?" I was getting used to the term.

"Yes, we usually stopped for a break at Callander and had something to eat. Later on we would eat sandwiches I had made up."

"Thoughtful girl," I chuckled, and she gave me an appreciative smile.

We did as she and the old man had done before, stopping at the busy little town, and having found a parking space, made for the same small café where they had previously eaten.

After our meal, I sat back taking in the hustle and bustle of the café; waitresses never halting to draw breath, clearing tables and rushing back to bring an order from the kitchen.

One such approached our table. "Enjoy the meal?" she asked, lifting our empty plates on to a tray.

"Very much," Sue answered, smiling up at her. "Is it always as busy?" she asked nodding around her.

"Pretty much in the summer."

I held up the photo of 'Gramps.' "I don't suppose with so many coming and going you would remember having seen this old man by any chance?"

The woman studied it for a moment or two, then shook her head. "There's so many people coming and going, you scarcely have time to notice."

I nodded. "I quite understand."

"Run off your feet, I would say," Sue added sympathetically.

"You can say that again." Then she was away, taking our dirty dishes to the kitchen, to repeat the same old thing again…and again.

Leaving the bustling little town behind, I headed for Lochearnhead, Crianlarich, and then on to Tyndrum.

"We might have better luck here at Tyndrum. With old Jock being on his own, he may well have stopped here for a bite instead of Callander. Or if not, there is every possibility that he might have stopped at one of the hotels further on, as they will be quieter than the average café or restaurant," I suggested hopefully.

Sue studied my face as if it had 'clown' tattooed on it.

" How do propose doing that, we have only just eaten?

"Perks of the trade," I laughed. "No, you can wait in the car while I make some discreet local inquiries."

"It might cost you a drink or two to find out, and if so I had better do the driving," she suggested with an amused smile.

"Never. Geraldine is too temperamental to let anyone else handle her."

"Geraldine!" Sue howled with laughter. "Is this what you call it?"

"Wheest, she'll hear you. The last thing is for her to go in the huff, and leave us stranded here," I replied in mock alarm, as I got out of the car.

A few minutes later I was back.

"No luck?" Sue said, reading my expression.

"Only a little."

"What do you mean 'only a little;"?

"Well, the headwaiter in one of the hotels remembers, 'Gramps' but that was when he called here two or three months back. He remembers him as a good tipper."

"Oh. Better luck next time," Sue sighed as I started up the car.

We had better luck with our questions with the receptionist at The Grand Hotel, in Fort William.

"Yes I remember the old chap, he is quite a regular here. Quite a character, too," the young man smiled, as if recollecting a previous encounter.

"When was the last time you saw, Mr Fraser?" I asked.

The man gave a twist of his lip as if the action would help him remember. "Last week I think it was."

"Could you be more precise? Perhaps look up your register?" The way I had asked the questions had the young man stare at me as if I had said something rude.

"I should say that would breach Company policy."

Now I knew I had his hackles up, and he would tell me hang all.

Sue came to my rescue. "It really is important. You see Mr Fraser has not contacted us in a while, and we are naturally concerned that something may have happened to him, you understand."

She was good I thought, the way her voice took on that little girl lost affect, and the pleading eyes.

For a moment the receptionist hesitated, and I could see that Sue had already won him over, and it was only his hurt pride that prevented him from swinging immediately to his computer. He gave a sigh of resignation as if this was indeed a great service he was rendering us, and we should not underestimate the risk he was taking on our behalf, and as his eyes fell to the screen I heard the sound of rapidly tapped keys.

"Mr Fraser was with us for three days." He gave the arrival and departure dates, and looked up at me from the screen as if to say, 'am I a genius or am I not?

"Was he alone?" I asked, and heard a sharp intake of breath from Sue.

The genius shot me a short sharp look which suggested I had gone beyond proper protocol.

"If he was by himself, he might have taken ill somewhere. He liked to hill-walk you will understand." Now it was my turn to be the genius.

The young man glanced at the screen. "Yes he was sir." His eyes bore into me, daring me to ask further.

"Thank you," Sue replied before I could. "That was very kind of you."

Unfortunately for me we had two separate rooms. No surprise here of course.

Before we met for dinner, I took the opportunity to phone my brother Fenton.

"How's it going big man?" I asked cheerily of him.

"Bit dull. Not much doing." He sounded bored.

"Perhaps I could change that," I said. "I am up here at Fort William on a case and my clients have asked me to try and locate an old friend of theirs who has gone walkabout. He has done this sort of thing before, and at present they don't want the police involved. They believe he is in the Loch Arkaig area. So, Fenton should you come across an abandon car with, or without an old man in it, perhaps you could let me know?"

"Not much to go on, brother, there are probably dozens of old codgers up here stoating about as if lost...I think it is something to do with the midgies. However, I will see what I can do without losing my pension. I'll get back to you on your mobile, if that's all right."

"Fine I replied." We talked about the weather, his job etc. before wishing him all the best, and I switched off my mobile.

After our showers.. again separate, we met in the dining room. Sue wore a neat dress, with a floral cardigan, and I a dark blue suit. Sue seemed impressed.

"I didn't think you would dress for dinner."

"Nor I you," I replied, returning her smile.

"This little thing?" She pulled down the sleeves of her cardigan, with a chuckle. "Gramps gave it to me on our last trip up here."

"He must think a good deal of you," I said lifting the menu.

"Sympathy mostly."

I raised my eyebrows.

"He gave me the job because I was out of work. I might have all the right qualifications for something better than a secretary, but how to obtain one is the question. We might have many students with degrees here in Scotland, but we still have to send to Poland for a plumber, if you take my meaning."

"Touché" I said. "But why sympathy?"

She gave a shrug. "I believe Gramps thinks he owes it to the family. But, please don't ask me why, as I honestly do not know." Her look and tone told me to desist.

It had rained during the night; no surprise, as this was the Scottish Highlands and they had not signed up for global warming. We headed for my car in the hotel parking lot, and just as we had almost reached my car, Sue slipped on the wet gravel. Throwing out a hand to prevent herself from falling, she scraped her arm on the grill of the nearest car, and landed with a thud.

"Sue!" I exclaimed as I ran forward to help her to her feet. "Are you all right?" Why do people ask such stupid questions of people when clearly they are not I thought?

She looked up at me, and tried to smile. "Stupid me, I should have watched where I was going."

"Better have a look at that." I pointed to her arm.

"I will be all right, it's just a scratch as they say in the movies."

"Just the same I think we should mosey over to the corral and make sure it's ok." I suggested in my best John Wayne accent.

Sue rubbed her arm and gave me a grin. "Mosey over to the OK Corral, you mean?

"Yip. A man's got to do what a man's got to do," I said, and taking her other arm guided her out of the parking lot and across the road to the square, and so to the chemist shop.

Sue took off her waterproof jacket, and rolled up her sleeve to let the pharmacist take a look, explaining how it had happened.

"It's not too bad. I'll give it a clean and bandage it up. Just make sure you don't get it infected. I'll also give you some cream," the woman in the white coat said.

It was when we had finished and Sue had pulled on her jacket that I saw her draw in a deep breath. At first I thought that she might be in pain, until I saw that she was looking at a well dressed man in his mid thirties who had just entered the shop.

He saw her looking at him, and grinning broadly walked to meet her. "Well fancy meeting you here of all places, and at this time."

"I could say the same to you." Sue's response was cold.

"You think your promotion will save you?" he asked.

"Guaranteed. Even should it not, it is not the end of MacDonald Fraser," she said bitterly.

The man gave a lopsided grin. "I would not bet on it. However, I bid you a good day, Sue, and I wish MacDonald Fraser the very best." With this he took his leave, giving me a slight nod of acknowledgment as he did so. The encounter had been short, but far from sweet.

We were in the car and driving out of Fort William before Sue offered an explanation.

"That was the dreaded Millar MacKay. His daddy owned an Export, Import business in Leith. Now he runs it in partnership with a man called Jack Gray, not a very nice individual. They both have shown a keen interest in the distillery."

"I got the impression that you didn't seem to think much of Mr MacKay."

"I don't."

I nodded my understanding and turned left at the roundabout that would take me on to the road to Corpach, and I would have missed the 'B' road we were to take to Loch Arkaig had not Sue instructed me to turn at the canal, and the 'Neptune's Staircase.'

Eventually we reached Achnasaul on the twisting one track road, which one time was at the water's edge, the next hidden from the loch itself by a screen of trees, before once again dipping down to the loch side.

"Do you come here often?" I asked, drawing into a passing place to let a car full of tourist past."

"That's the strangest chat up line I've ever heard!" Sue let out a peal of laughter.

I felt myself blush. "It wasn't supposed to be, really."

Sue drew me a look. "Not good enough for you, Mr Detective," she chuckled.

I felt myself blush even deeper. "It is not the done thing to cohort with clients," I said as a means of escaping the situation. Then we both laughed.

"Now back to my original question," I prompted her.

"Oh, the last time we came here? I believe it was March, and boy was it cold. I don't know how Gramps could stick it. He had this map he had made, all grids and squares in order to keep track where he has searched. He and the elder MacDonald have been at it since the forties."

We were on the loch side before I was truly aware of the enormity of the task the two old pals had set themselves. It would have taken the entire population of Fort William working flat out, and on overtime to truly search the entire length of the loch, not including the surrounding hillside.

We were a little past where a few rowing boats bobbed about in the water before Sue spoke again. She pointed to a grey two storey house sitting a little way back from the loch shore. "Gramps usually calls in there to say hello to Ewen Cameron the gamekeeper, before he heads further up the loch."

"We best do the same," I said slowing down and turning into the gutted driveway.

"We can always ask him when he last saw the old man."

As we approached the house, a man of medium height came out of the door. I would have guessed him to be in his mid fifties, sporting a grey beard which I had to confess suited him. For a moment his face registered curiosity at this strange car, until as we drew closer, he recognised Sue and gave her a wave of welcome.

"Ewen," Sue cried cheerfully as she got out of the car.

"If it is not wee Sue, herself." The man's face lit up at the sight of his unexpected guest. "What brings you to Cour House?" He drew closer peering into the car, and his eyes passed me, still searching. "Where is the old one today?"

"That's what we came to ask you Ewen."

I got out of the car and closed the door, waiting for Sue to introduce me.

"Gramps has been missing for over a week now. Oh, sorry, this is Mr West Barns who we have engaged to find Gramps."

"Aye." The man studied me as if considering if I was up to the job or not.

"Pleased to make your acquaintance, Mr Cameron," I said across the car.

Ewen nodded. "You will come away in and we can have a word or two over… I was about to say dram, but as you are driving you can both settle for tea." He turned and escorted us to the house.

The interior was rough, but not shabby, and smelled of animals, a few I expected just passing through to pastures new. A Border Collie that suddenly appeared was not one of the latter I believed, as it gave me a growl before making itself comfortable on the couch.

"Put the kettle on, Craig, we have visitors," Ewen called out to someone 'ben' the house. He motioned us to take a seat. "That's Craig, my nephew," he explained. "He comes to bide with me for a wee while during his school summer holidays. Now, what is this you were saying about the 'old one?'" he asked sitting down on the couch and stroking the dog's ear.

Sue enlightened him. "Gramps has been missing since last Wednesday. Well that is the last time we heard from him. We thought he might have called in here as he usually does, so we came to ask you."

Ewen nodded. "He was here right enough, but it was Tuesday of last week not Wednesday as you say. Not his usual self, the old man. A bit down after Archie's passing, I would say. Both of them have been coming here more years that I care to remember. Aye, even from the time my own father was gamekeeper."

"Did he go up the loch as usual?" Sue asked, before I could.

"Aye, but he never stopped on the way back. That's unless he called when I was up the hillside."

Before any further questions could be asked, a young lad of about fifteen or so appeared, carrying a tray with two mugs and a plate of biscuits.

"Craig, could you not have brought out the good china for our new guest here?" Ewen said chastising the boy in mock annoyance.

"A mug is apt for me, Mr Cameron." I gave the man my best smile, as I had the feeling I should have to solicit his help.

Suddenly his demeanour changed towards me. "You are helping Sue to find old Jock, instead of the police?"

Sue answered for me. "Yes, we have asked him to Ewen, as we don't know as yet what has happened to the old soul. Should he merely be lying low so to speak to recover from Archie's death and to find the strength to meet our potentials buyers at our promotion, it would not help our sales should the press get hold of it and misconstrue the facts. You know what lengths reporters will go to, to get a story."

"Aye. And that's a fact. However, Jock cannot be further up the loch without someone coming upon his car. Even that is, that he passed here with the express intention of not letting me know. And this being so, why?"

Sue clasped her mug of tea in her lap, unsure if she should say what was in her mind. She looked first at the man then the boy, suddenly as if having decided, she said, "Gramps sent me a text. He said 'I have found it.'"

Ewen stared at her in disbelief. "You don't mean Charlie's gold? After all those years of searching he has finally found it, and here was me thinking that the greedy clansmen had already divided it out amongst themselves. What do you think of that Craig?" he asked the boy, giving the dog a slap in delight.

"More history to learn," the boy sighed.

I laughed at his expression. "You don't like history I take it?"

"Not when they keep changing it," he replied sorrowfully.

Ewen rose, the gesture saying he had other things to attend to. "As I believe it is your intention to head further up the loch where the old man has been searching, I can show you where. Craig, you come with me and Shep in the Land Rover, you can help them, while I go to the hill. My, oh my the old bugger has finally found it," he chuckled.

"The boy does not look too pleased," I said as I followed the Land Rover.

"Would you be at his age?" Sue said as we bumped our way on the rutted road.

"Don't know, but I can wait to find out," I laughed.

Sue's drew me a look. "Do you mean physically or mentally?" she asked with a grin.

"Mentally, I suppose," I sighed, as the Land Rover drew to a halt.

Ewen got out as we did and he walked towards us. "This is where old Jock brought his car last time I saw him here, when I was up there." He pointed to hillside above.

"I would leave you the dog, but I have something else in mind for him, today."

"It's all right Ewen. Thanks for your time, and I am sure Craig's help will be invaluable." She gave the boy a smile.

"Only if he keeps awake. I have never known a laddie to sleep so much. Sometimes I think he is for the hibernating. Come Shep let us be on our way." So saying, Ewen lifted his bag and shotgun from the back of his vehicle and started off.

"Where do you suggest we start looking, Craig?"

The way the girl had said it had the boy look at her as if she were treating him as a grown up, and not a mere schoolboy. I saw his eyes roam over her as if aware of her for the first time, and I felt an unwarranted flash of jealousy.

"I think Mr Fraser would search higher up the hillside." The boy looked at us each in turn, before saying a little softer. "Someone would have seen him should he be lying anywhere near the loch side." And at Sue's gasp, realising what he had said, added a little softer, "Or maybe he is not anywhere here at all, and just fine."

"Then let's start from here," Sue suggested. "It's as good a place as any." She went round to the boot of the car and took out a haversack. "A flask and sandwiches," she explained.

"Let me carry it for you," Craig eagerly volunteered. And I knew he was now pleased that he had come. I was not. Beside the seriousness of the situation I wished to have this girl to myself for the day.

"Are you all right for climbing in those?" I asked the boy, pointing to his trainers. He was attired in jeans and a white T-shirt, the logo which said 'New York.'

"I'll be fine," he answered and turned to the climb.

We searched for the remainder of the morning, with the boy covering most of the ground. I myself was suffering; too many runs in the car instead of runs on my feet.

"I think, Sue needs a rest," I said using the girl as an excuse. To my relief and delight, Sue agreed.

I had not been completely aware of having fallen asleep after our afternoon snack. Sue lay on the grass her head resting on her haversack. Craig had taken off his T-shirt and lay asleep, and I envied him his sun tan, and thought again of my own peely wally skin. I would have to do something about my fitness or lack of it; this fifteen year old was showing me up.

I looked across at Sue, she was truly lovely and I felt my heart beat faster. She saw me looking at her and smiled.

"Where do we go from here?" She rose and stifled a yawn.

"Better ask our scout," I suggested pointing to the sleeping boy.

Sue acknowledged my suggestion and crossed to shake Craig by the arm. "Come on sleepy head, we have work to do."

It took a little time for the boy to stir, but as soon as he saw who had shaken him, he quickly became fully awake.

"Where do you think we should look now, Craig?" Sue asked smiling down at him.

Craig got hurriedly to his feet, sleep forgotten. "Further up the hillside towards, Loch Blair, Sue."

"OK kid, let's go."

At the end of the day we were both pretty tired; well Sue was pretty, I was just tired, with Craig showing us up by whistling as we walked back to my car.

Once back at Cour House, Ewen came to the door as we got out of the car.

"I thought you all had got lost, you have been away for hours. I have made a bite or two for you to eat." He turned to go inside, throwing over his shoulder as he did so. "And you best get to the sandwiches before his lordship here does, it's like living with a Piranha, so it is."

Although the heat of the June day had cooled, I still struggled to keep my eyes open as I bit into my sandwich, and lifted what felt like a two ton mug of tea.

"You had no luck, I should think?" Ewen sat on a chair by the unlit fire.

Sue put down her cup and shook her head. "I hope Gramps is not lying out there and we failed to find him," she said sadly, as if we could have done better.

"No sign of his car of course? I thought not. He might not be here on Arkaig side at all." Ewen looked at me from across the room, as if expecting me to explain to the girl what was already forming in my mind, and no doubt in his mind as well.

Sue saw his expression and turned to me. For a moment I sat there thinking on what I was about to say, focusing my attention on Craig sitting on the floor, stroking the dog.

"What Ewen means, Sue, is since there is no car here, how could old Jock come to be here at all."

"But Gramps text said he had found it," the girl said in exasperation.

"Found what, Sue?" Ewen broke in. "That does not mean he has found Bonnie Prince Charlie's treasure. It could mean anything."

"What else could it mean," she answered defiantly. "He must be here. This is where he believed the treasure to be."

I knew she was getting close to breaking point, and what I was about to suggest was not going to help any.

"Look at it this way Sue," I began. "In order for 'Gramps' to make the journey here he would have to come by car, and since we did not find any car, someone else must have brought him." Sue's head jerked up and she stared at me as I asked, "Would the old man have mentioned his find to anyone else?"

"No!" Sue almost shouted the word and the dog's ears cocked and he let out a low growl, as if to say ' mind your manners or you're oot.' "The only one interested in Gramps, fascination for the treasure was old Archie, and since he is dead," she gestured helplessly.

Suddenly her expression changed as if having arrived at the same conclusion as Ewen and myself. "He's dead. That's what you are trying to say."

I spread my hands in a gesture meant to reassure her in some way. "Let's say for arguments sake that someone did bring him by car, which no one here heard passing by…again that is if the treasure is beyond this point at all. Old Jock showed this person the hiding place of the treasure…"

"And they murdered him for it!" Sue cried. She was on her feet, and the dog rose to stare up at her, unable in its own canine mind as to what this girl was on about.

I had made a mess of it, now there was no going back. "If Old Jock did show this person the treasure and wanted to steal it for himself, then he had no alternative but to silence the old man." Sue gave a moan and collapsed back into her seat. Ewen gave me a slight nod telling me to go on. "So Gramps, as you call the old man could still be lying where the treasure is. Since no one has previously found this place…say it is a cave for example for almost three hundred years, then there is every reason that this person will leave the old man there. However, he cannot leave the treasure where it is, this he must move so as not to incriminate himself. As I have said, as no one is likely to find this cave, he can afford to wait six months, a year or even two before he moves it bit by bit to a new location where he can then announce his find to the world."

"And Gramps will lie there for how many hundred years?" Sue shuddered. "But who else was hunting for the treasure? No one that I know of, so he must have confided in someone he knew and trusted." Sue's face turned a deathly white as she realised what she had just said.

"I think we should leave it there, Sue. If you care to, we can start afresh in the morning. That's of course if our chief scout, Tonto, is willing?"

Craig rose. "What time will you be here?" he asked, his question directed solely at Sue.

"Not too early, or Tonto here will not be able to prevent the wagons from being massacred," Ewen suggested.

Not to be outdone, Craig responded with a grin. "Well, everyone knows Indians don't fight in the dark."

"Then you've no hope since it's almost mid- summer." Ewen gave his nephew a playful slap on the back.

"We'll breakfast at the hotel, and be here around half past nine."

"That's the middle of the night to you, Craig," Ewen scoffed.

The boy made a face, at his uncle's quip. Then his young face lit up. "Not to worry Sue, I'll be here."

Once in the car, to lighten Sue's mood I said, "You have an admirer there."

Sue gave a grunt. "That's nice, I don't have too many."

"Perhaps you should get out more often, and meet people." I attempted to make light of it.

"People like yourself no doubt." She half turned to look at me and I did not know whether she was mocking me or not.

"You could do worse…not much, but maybe a bit or so."

"I'll think about it."

So we left it at that.

Somehow I think we were both glad to be back by the loch next day. Our conversations in the hotel were slightly stilted, although after a couple of whiskies Sue began to forget her troubles and mellow a little. However, it was evident that she was deeply troubled by the disappearance of old Jock, and who could blame her.

She put down her mobile. "I can't get a signal from here. Simon texted me at the hotel this morning, he wants to know when I am coming back as there is so much to do for the promotion. He did say he wanted me back in a couple of days."

"Do you want to?" I asked and hoped not, as I believed our relationship could, and would flourish after all this was over.

"It would mean me taking a train back if you intend to continue your investigations here."

We were almost at the house again and I slowed the car a little in order to give myself time to think.

"Do you want to? Or should I say, do you have to?"

"Simon can be a beast when it comes to work…my work. I am only a secretary after all, and he is part owner of a large Company."

"I have the feeling that you don't have much time for 'cold eyes.'"

"Cold eyes?" She stared at me and wrinkled her brows.

"Sorry, Mr Simon MacDonald," I laughed.

"'Cold Eyes,' what a gorgeous name for him." And for the first time she laughed heartedly. "No, I really could do with a day or two away from that lot. Even when he sent me to York, he was always on the phone. Eventually I had to switch it off to get some peace, and I phoned him instead when I thought I had to."

"Do the same here, I'll back you up. I'll tell him we were captured by wild Highlanders who asked for a ransom of ten sheep and a distillery."

Again her laughter was warm as she said, "Ok I'll stay. But remember he's your employer too."

Craig was at the door awaiting our arrival, his eyes seeking out Sue as he ran to meet the car.

"That's the first morning since he came here, Sue, that I have not had to pull him out of bed," Ewen chuckled as we came in.

Craig's face turned a deep red. "Well at least I have something to get up for, it makes a difference from feeding chickens, and those other things you have me doing all day to keep me happy."

"Just say when you wish to leave young Craig, and I will have your P45 all ready and waiting."

"Wages as well?" Craig asked, tickling the dog's ear.

"Seems I'm not the only one with employer troubles," Sue grinned at the boy, enjoying the good natured banter.

"Where do you suggest we look today?" I asked Ewen, acknowledging him as the authority here.

"Craig told me where you were yesterday, so I have advised him where to look today. I should be up around there somewhere myself today."

"If you are not too late, you might even get a cup of coffee from us." Sue made the offer with a grin.

"I'll hold you to it," Ewen answered, giving Sue the thumbs up.

It was well past a mile or so from where we had parked the car yesterday that we began what was to me a fruitless search, and I had to remind myself that I was being handsomely paid for it.

"I think we should rest a wee bit, Craig," I suggested, my eyes on the retreating backside of Craig as we toiled up the steep hillside.

"Yes, Craig," Sue agreed flopping down on the dry grass. "You forget Gramps was nearing his eighties. I don't think he would have made the climb."

Craig rested against a rock. He pointed upwards. "Maybe not, Sue, but he could have made it up yonder by coming at it from Loch Blair, though it is a fair walk if he was to trek from Murlaggan. Perhaps we could try again tomorrow? Or if you like I can go on a bit further up?" He stood up in preparation of climbing higher.

I chewed a piece of grass and rested my eyes not on Sue but on the haversack, as Craig was carrying its contents of coffee and sandwiches.

"No, Craig, "I think we have done enough climbing for today. Anyhow, according to legend, the treasure is by the loch side, not away up here," Sue explained.

"Aye, I suppose so," Craig nodded in agreement. "It could also well be that the treasure lies on the other side of the loch itself." He reinforced his argument by continuing. "And the landscape would also be different than it is today."

"Gramps and Archie have searched yon side too. I remember Gramps saying, that they were convinced that the treasure lies on this side. But where, is another matter."

Our sandwiches eaten we started down for the loch side. Craig, the first to reach the shore, lifted a pebble and threw it into the steel grey water, and |I envied him his stamina.

Sue sat down on a rock by the water's edge. She gave a shiver. "I think it's going to rain." She looked up at a sky rapidly losing its blue to black and dull grey, and stood up on the rock, and Craig put out a hand to help her down.

It was then the shot rang out and I was aware of Craig shouting, "Uncle," at the same time as Sue toppled into the water.

"Jee- sus!" I swore and ran to where Craig had dived into the loch, and I cursed at never having learned to swim.

Sue had disappeared from sight and Craig was diving and resurfacing, drawing in great lung full's of air before diving in again. Again and again the boy dived and I thought Sue must have drowned.

I ran up and down like a headless chicken to where I thought and hoped she might resurface. Now and again I caught sight of Craig's white T-shirt before it too disappeared. Suddenly she was there, the water streaming from her hair as she seemed to rise out of the water, her panic stricken face registering horror and disbelief, in the arms of Craig who was vainly trying to bring her back to shore, one hand threshing water, the other holding on to the terrified girl.

Now at last there was something I could do. I ran to where Craig was heading for the shore, and I plunged into the water only too well aware of how cold it was as it seeped into my trousers and shoes. I got as far as waist deep and held out my hands to help.

As, if in a trance her face etched white, Sue threw out a hand and I grabbed it and with Craig now treading water managed to haul her to shore.

Together we managed to get the coughing choking girl on to a patch of grass where she sat shivering and staring wide eyed at both of us in turn. "I can't swim." She coughed again.

Now there was something I could do, and not leave everything to this young Tarzan here. I quickly took off my sweater and handed it to her. "Here put this on, you're freezing." Her hands shook as she took the sweater and I helped her to pull it over her head.

"You're all right you haven't been hit?" My eyes roamed over the soaked girl.

She shook her head, and still shivering, she looked up at Craig standing there wringing out his soaked T-shirt, and shakily got to her feet.

"Come here, hero. You saved my life." She clutched the embarrassed but delighted boy to her bosom, and I hated the kid even more.

"It was nothing Sue, I would do the same again," he mumbled still wrapped in the girl's embrace.

Yes I thought- and again and again if you were to receive a hug like that every time you lucky bas…. At the realization that Sue had not been hit, the tension slowly ebbed from my body, until I saw the bruise on the side of her head and instantly understood how close the shot had been.

"What's going on here?"

None of us had heard the gamekeeper approach.

"Sue fell in the water, Uncle!" Craig cried out, now free from Sue's embrace.

Ewen looked at his nephew, then at Sue then back again to the boy. "Put your shirt on laddie, you'll catch your death," he commanded.

Sue stepped forward. "There was a gunshot, and I was knocked into the water."

"You are not hurt are you, Sue?" The man said it a way as if it was an everyday occurrence.

"But she could have been, Uncle!" Craig leapt to the defence of the one he secretly admired.

"We heard a shot. A rifle shot." I looked at the gun the man was holding, surprised that the gun he carried was not a shotgun.

"Aye, that would be mine right enough, though I had no reason to fire it in your direction; even less to try and hurt Sue. Come on, less of this talk and let us get these two wet kippers back to the house. Craig, you come with me in the Rover. Here take my jacket, you are fair shivering laddie. If you come down with anything, your mother will kill me, and that's a fact."

Following the Land Rover back to the house, Sue said through her chattering teeth. "Perhaps it was the shock of the gun going off that made me fall off the rock. Ewen didn't seem to take what happened too seriously."

"This time you will tell the police." I thumped the steering wheel. "Now it's more than just looking for a missing old man!" I was angry and not a little frustrated as well as afraid for this lovely young girl.

"No!" Her cry startled me, and I momentarily lost my grip on the steering wheel.

"You will!" I shouted back at her.

"You can't make me, I am your client!"

I shook my head. "Wrong. Mr and Mrs MacDonald, your employers, are my clients."

"That's why I can't go to the police. They will kill me if I do. I don't mean that literally. But you know what I mean."

"I know that someone almost has," I threw back at her.

"Please, West, give it to the end of the week. I'm sure Gramps will turn up. The MacDonalds, particularly Simon, will not be best pleased if I have gone to the police and the old man was to turn up: especially after the Press have got a hold of it."

I held my hands up in exasperation before dropping them back on to the wheel.

"Suit yourself, woman, but don't come running to me if you get yourself killed."

Sue gave a cackle of a laugh. "O.k. it's a promise." She shivered. "Now to get out of these clothes."

"Now there I can help,"

"Cheeky," she said and laughed again.

I was in the shower when the thought struck me. Not a good place to be struck, I thought with a smile; my only smile, for, as I thought it over, it now started to make sense…or some of it did. Sue had said that if Gramps were to tell anyone about finding the treasure, it would be to someone he knew and trusted. Then who better than Ewen Cameron?

After Sue's little dip in the loch we had returned to Cour House where, Sue, had donned a spare pair of Craig's jeans and T-shirt which she said she would have washed and ironed by the hotel where he could pick them up in a day or two, much to the boy's disappointment, as he had hoped his idol would have remained longer. As for me, the boy wouldn't mind if I went home today, if not before.

Sue had also enclosed a thank you card with a small gift of money. And I was sure that card would be under the boy's pillow every night, or maybe on it.

My thoughts returned to what had happened at the house, and how I had found it hard to be civil to the gamekeeper, although Sue seemed to have taken the line that the sudden crack of the gun going off had simply made her slip, and it had been her own fault.

Yet to me it made sense. If the old man had told the gamekeeper about his find, and had taken him to where the treasure was hidden, and the sight of all that gold had made the gamekeeper think of having it for himself, he would have had no option but to kill the old man. Also, there was no one in a better position than he to transport the gold to some other spot, where after a time he could 'accidentally' stumble upon it, and also claim the fame that would come with it. I snapped my fingers in satisfaction and dropped the soap.

Now it all made sense. With Ewen living on the spot, so to speak, he could move the gold at his leisure to its new location; somewhere of course where no one was likely to find it until he himself made it public. And as regards to the place itself where the gold had lain hidden undisturbed for more than two hundred years, it was never likely to be discovered again, for another two hundred years or so. Therefore, old Jock would lie in peace there. Or would he? I shuddered when I thought about what I had heard about restless spirits. Thinking about spirits I could down one right now, or maybe even two.

As I dressed, my theory began to unravel slightly, or even a big bit. Why would Ewen Cameron want to kill Sue? Should Sue have chosen to go to the police and tell them of the incident, it would have drawn unwanted attraction to himself; something which he must avoid at all costs. And had he killed her, it would have created even more attention to himself.

I shrugged into my jacket in preparation of going downstairs to meet the subject of controversy in the dining room. Did Sue unwittingly know something, however innocently that Ewen must prevent her from disclosing? Suddenly I wished I was back home searching for Mrs MacKenzie's dog: that at least was uncomplicated… and a lot safer as well; unless I were to meet the old lady herself. But what could Sue possibly know? She had said that everything that was important to Gramps was in his safe and he had the only key, not even his solicitor had one. The spare too, she believed was also well hidden. Perhaps in the safe lay the answer to this mystery.

CHAPTER TWO

Next day, back home once more, I pushed open my office door against the bumph lying on the floor; mostly flyers and catalogues. I threw them on my desk and pressed the button on my answering machine. One call sounded promising, it was a divorce case. Compared to what I was doing at present this would be boring, but safe. The next call was brief and to the point, it was old Mrs MacKenzie. "Where have you been Barns? And what aboot my wee dog ye lazy .." at this point the phone had terminated in bleeps, but happily not from the lady. Old people I sighed, they cannot cope with such technology.

I had just sat down at my desk and was savouring the prospect of sauntering down the corridor to make myself a coffee when the phone rang again. Believing it to be Sue, I hastily picked it up a smile already on my face. Instead, "Hello you, is that you West Barns? Where have ye been gallivanting off to now? Ma wee dog could be deed by now,ye lazy devil."

"Hello Mrs MacKenzie, I have been away contacting Interpol about your wee dog. They have dropped everything and are on your case right now."

"Don't get smart with me boy," came the reply. "No' even as much as a poster on a lamppost."

"Well, Mrs MacKenzie, I didn't think posters on a lamppost would be of much help considering there are not many dogs in North Berwick that I know of that can read."

"I'll gie ye read, ye cheeky devil! My wee dog could have been stolen and flown out the country by this time."

"Only if it was an Airedale, Mrs MacKenzie," I chuckled.

However the old lady on the other end was in no mood for hilarity. "It's you that will need a plane oot the country if I get a haud o' ye West Barns. Ye are no' a patch on yer brother Fenton." The phone went down with a bang.

My instincts told me that I should pay a visit to the distillery and find out how the promotion was faring. It was Friday, the first day open to the public and the place was thriving with people either sauntering from tent to tent or rushing about as if the items on sale would quickly vanish. On one corner of the field, marquees, furnished with the usual refreshments for hungry customers, or the curious and hungry, were doing a roaring trade. One such marquee held all the tartan paraphernalia one could imagine, kilts - jackets – sporrans - hose - sgian cubhs' - plaids, all of the best quality. Already I heard a multitude of different accents as I made for the office in the distillery itself.

A kind guide pointed me to the main office and then set about helping others. As I drew closer I was aware of Amanda and her husband in what appeared to be a heated argument, the sound of which the glass panelling failed to prevent leaking, or should that be screeching out.

I heard Simon shout, "And don't try to deny it, I saw you with him last night in old Jock's office of all places."

Amanda, about to reply, saw me and her face lit up, probably with relief rather than joy at seeing me. "Ah, Mr Barns we have or, Sue rather, has just received a text from Jock. Seemingly he is, or was staying up at Laggan and is on his way here. Quite a relief, don't you think? Now I suppose we can dispense with your services." She gave me a disarming smile.

"A waste of time and money if you ask me," Simon snorted.

"I'm glad the old man is all right. However, I should like to hang around until he actually turns up," I replied.

"You mean that way you'll earn a little bit more."

I had just about enough of cold eyes, but I held my tongue. No use antagonising Mr Know- it- all, at least not until I got paid. Instead I asked where I might find Sue, and followed Amanda's directions where to go…had it been left to Simon, he would also have told me where to go, and that several degrees hotter than it was outside.

Sue was working in old Jock's office, and she appeared to be up to her neck in work. She saw me and instantly her expression changed from one of exasperation to one of joy… or something close to it.

"I got a text this morning from Gramps, he is alive and well! Is that not the best of news? All that worrying for nothing. He was.."

"I know," I interrupted, curbing her enthusiasm, "Amanda, told me."

"So he will be here sometime today or tomorrow." She let out a sigh of relief. "Neil has been coping as best he can. He can do the job relatively well, but it's Gramps the overseas buyers want to deal with. He knows most of them from his overseas trips."

Sue was rapidly shuffling papers from one pile to another as she spoke. "Simon must think I am an octopus, the amount of work he has me doing. He has been so angry at me for going away with you, and letting all this work pile up." She pointed to the paperwork on the desk.

"Sue," I said drawing closer. "I don't think old Jock will turn up, so don't get your hopes up."

It was as if I had slapped her face. Her face turned a bright red, and her eyes blazed angrily at me. "But I got a text from him this morning. He has been up at Laggan. Seemingly he couldn't get a message from his mobile." Her voice was filled with desperation.

"Do you honestly think those messages you received since his disappearance have actually come from him? No message you say, because of no signal? What about landline telephones? Usually these still work, even in the remotest of Highland glens."

Sue dropped the folder she had been holding. "You think, Gramps is dead? You think someone has murdered him." She had trouble saying the word, as if by doing so she would have to face the inevitable. "But why? If so who do you think killed him?"

"My bet is Ewen Cameron." I followed this by explaining my reasons.

"But Ewen and Gramps were friends, as was Ewen's father before him!" The look on Sue's face told me she thought this was hard to believe and that I was just a detective who had difficulty in finding a stray dog, much less finding an old man.

"There is more to it than that, and I am determined to find out, unless of course you want to tell the police?"

Sue shook her head, and I felt a snake in the grass…or some other low life at the way I had changed this previously frustrated but happy girl, to what she was now the way she looked at me, then as if to convince herself more than me, she said, "Gramps will be here. Just you wait and see. So if you don't mind Mr Barns I have work to do."

To say I was cut to my polished black shoes would be an understatement. Sue deliberately did not look up from her work as I stood there not knowing what else to say or do to convince her that the mobile messages did not come from her beloved Gramps, and that the old man was already dead, and as far as I was concerned the police should be called in. I turned round and left the office and the busy girl to her work.

By Saturday afternoon I had plucked up enough courage to return to the promotion, with the intention of patching things up with Sue. Perhaps, if I were to ask her out for a meal after she finished work it might help, and it might lead to something further. She had not called me in order to contradict me about Gramps not being dead, so I took it the old man had not made an appearance as the text had said he would.

Once again as I passed Simon's office there was some sort of disagreement, this time with a tall deeply tanned gentleman whose guttural tones seeping through the glass panelling told me he was either German or Austrian. Seeping might not be the correct word, for as the conversation escalated I gathered this Germanic gentleman was not best pleased by the replies Simon appeared to be giving him.

I walked on, but much to my disappointment Sue was not in her office. When I passed Simon's office again his visitor had gone, and Simon was sitting staring at me, or through me rather. Then I saw him close his eyes and hold his head in his hands, an object of utter dejection.

Outside, the grounds were a hive of activity, and although I had searched every tent pavilion and marquee, I still had not found Sue. I was also loath to ask his nibs, Simon Cold Eyes, aware of the mood he was in when last I saw him. Reluctantly, as there was nothing I could do here, and my vision of having the girl to myself had gone down the drain; as it had on many other occasions with others of the opposite sex, I decided to leave.

It was as I was walking to the parking place that I almost bumped into Millar Mackay, who I had first encountered in the pharmacy in Fort William.

"Ah! Nice to see you again." He gave me a cheery smile. "You do remember me? You were with Sue Lovat."

I said, "of course, although we were never formally introduced."

"Millar Mackay." He held out his hand.

I shook it saying, "West Barns."

"You are a friend of Sue's, I take it?"

"Something like that. Although, I haven't seen her today amongst all this crowd." I gestured to the chattering people around me. "I should say it's a great success, don't you think?"

Millar MacKay gave me a smile that suggested my naivety. "A very grand attendance I grant you, but very little sales. Oh, there are plenty scurrying about, and no doubt some buying the odd bargain here and there, but it is the big sales that really count, and buyers want to deal with the top man himself, whom they know, but he does not appear to be here. I wonder why? As it is a matter of life and death to the Company, I really cannot understand why he has failed to be present." Millar MacKay gave a chuckle. "Maybe the old fellow has succumbed to his own produce or something worse." He was about to move off when he added, "Simon should have taken my offer, now that Jock Fraser is…"

"Is what?" I asked controlling my anger at this snob.

"No offence old boy. I mean, that as the old man is not here, perhaps he is no longer able to cope. Neil Grant, is quite an adequate manager, but he doesn't know the overseas clients as old Jock did."

I noted MacKay's reference to old Jock in the past tense, but I said nothing as he bade me a fond farewell, or something like it.

I had no better success in finding Sue when I returned on Sunday afternoon. She had only briefly returned my text on Saturday to say she would be busy all day Sunday: an alternative to the old excuse women make to washing their hair. She still had made no reference to 'Gramps' non appearance. However, I made my way to the main building with the express purpose of trying to patch things up and make her see sense, and it was as I was doing so, that I recognised one of my old police colleagues coming out of the distillery.

"And what brings you here, Barns?" Thomson said to me. "And don't say your car. We are still recovering in the Force from your sense of humour." He gave me a smile saying that was his sense of humour.

"And what about your own? It's as dry as Orkney on a Sunday." I replied.

The smile playing on Thomson's face was one he usually reserved when taking statements. "Well, now that we have exchanged pleasantries, what are you doing here? I know your equally annoying brother Fenton likes his tipple, but I didn't know you did."

"Oh, I have been known to take a dram or two when I get annoyed, especially by humourless police officers."

"Point taken, you smart bas."

"I could ask you the same." I got my question in before he asked me again.

"Just routine." He saw by my look that I was not satisfied with his answer. "Don't you ever read the papers?

"Oor Wullie and the Broons, they're more real than some of the rubbish that passes as news these days."

"I won't argue with you there." He gave a little sigh as if having resigned himself in to telling me his reason for being here. Suddenly I had an unpleasant feeling in my gut, and I braced myself for what I was sure would be nothing other than bad news involving my clients.

"As I said, it's only routine. Last night we investigated the body of a man who had been found dead in a hotel in Edinburgh. At first glance, a robbery that went wrong appeared to be the motive."

"And now you're not so sure."

"We found his rented car outside, and in it were some papers in German. Turns out he was a journalist for some German newspaper. The only other item was a MacDonald Fraser, business card, that's why I am here. Strictly routine of course, there must be hundreds of folks with them, especially now." Thomson gestured at the crowd of people around him.

"And this guy," I felt my throat constrict a little as I asked the question; "I suppose he was murdered?"

Thomson nodded. "By a blunt instrument as they say." He gave me a suspicious look. "You wouldn't be able to help in any way would you West?"

"That rules me out, I can't play a blunt instrument." I gave him one of my most endearing smiles.

"There's that dry humour again. At least we only have one... no, make than none since your brother's up north to contend with back at Fettes. But all joking aside, you do know something, you're not just here for the view?"

I gave Bert Thomson my warmest smile. "Client confidentiality and all that old boy. However, when, and if I can, you will be the second to know."

Thomson took a step away. "No need for me to ask who the first will be. But it's my case Barns, not your brother Fenton's. This is not within his jurisdiction at the moment. Ok." With this far from warm brotherly officer warning ,we said our goodbyes.

Just when I had thought I had the case shut tight, it had sprung open on me and the contents were not much to my liking.

I had no doubt in my mind that the German gentleman I had seen in Simon's office, and who had been found dead in his hotel, could only be one and the same. But why? What connection if any had this to do with old Jock Fraser's disappearance? I turned away from the building now in no mood to face any of my clients and their associates. I needed time to think this over.

Monday morning saw me back in my office. My prospective client relating to a divorce who had phoned before, had not called back, and I was left to consider the possibility that they had either made up, or had shot one another. Therefore, it was fortunate that I had the MacDonald case to keep the wolf from the door.

However there was still old Mrs MacKenzie's dog to find. A week or so earlier, I had solicited the help of a group of local youngsters to help find the missing canine, with the added incentive of a reward of £25. Although I had told them emphatically, that the dog was a white Scotch Terrier, some had turned up next day with a few dogs big enough to put a saddle on, while others looked so tiny, offering me a paw with a bewildered expression on their faces as to why they had been dragged along here in the first place; the scene outside my office door reminiscent of the first day at Crufts, or auditions for Lassie.

I had decided to go along to the promotion later that evening, in the hope it would be quieter and I could have a word or so with Sue. However, by the time I got there, there were still a few of the public around. A security guard on one of the entrances was all set to deny me admission on the grounds they were now closing, and I had to persuade him to call the main office to verify who I was. When this had been done I drove to the main building, and was in the act of getting out of the car when a burst of light from one of the marquees caught my eye. I slammed the door shut and walked hurriedly towards a tent where flames were already soaring skywards. I broke into a run at the same time as I searched frantically around for help. An old couple, their backs to the blaze, were sauntering to their car completely oblivious as to what was behind them. "Get to your car!" I shouted as I ran towards them. Both looked at me as if I was daft, and I looked back as if I wasn't. "Behind you!" I bawled, and pointed. The old man turned round, and seeing what I meant took the old lady by the arm and they hurried as fast as their old legs would take them, as if having heard that their pensions had been doubled.

Now that the old couple were safe, I turned towards the fire. A few of the public who were still there, started running to their cars. Others, further away from the blaze, not yet aware of what was happening all around, remained browsing within some of the tents. I shouted to them as I passed on my way to the burning marquee, to get out as quickly as possible. I was still a little distance away from the blaze and wondering what on earth I could do, when suddenly my doubts were answered. With an ear shattering explosion the burning marquee exploded, hurtling me to the ground. A few yards closer and I would have been toast.

Now there seemed to be people scurrying all around: security men, staff, public and what appeared to be the distillery's own fire brigade running in all directions. A second explosion and another tent went up, flames leaping up into the dark blue sky. I hobbled to a wooden bench and stood leaning there, not knowing what best to do, when I heard the distant sound of a fire brigade's siren.

As I stood there, smoke began billowing in my direction and I decided to make my way back to the main building, as yet out of reach from the approaching fire. There was nothing I could do. It was then I saw a figure in one of the unaffected pavilions, and I thought at first it was to make sure no one was in there, until I saw the plastic can in his hand.

I started to run. Too late; he had spilled out the contents of the can and set fire to it. With a 'swoosh' the tent went up in flames, and I saw my arsonist run out one of the back entrances. I couldn't follow him through the blaze but instead tried to cut him off by rounding the side of the tent. He saw me and doubled back running parallel to the blazing tents. Coughing, I followed. At first I lost him amongst the smoke, and I held my hand up to shield my face from the raging heat. What the hell am I doing I thought? And who the hell am I chasing? I had not long to wait. He hit me as I rounded some flapping canvas not yet on fire, and I stumbled over a guy rope and went down. He raised his arm to hit me again as I struggled to my feet. Of all things it was a shepherd's crook that he had in his hand, and through the belching smoke I saw it rapidly descend in my direction.

The good Lord must have been on my side for once, for the crook became entangled in a guy rope as he brought it down, giving me just enough time to get to my feet, which I did with the speed of someone who has just heard that there was a sale on at B&Q. Choking and coughing, my eyes streaming from the smoke, I used the guy rope to shield me as I let out a punch to where his face should be. I missed, and he had the crook free. I grabbed it, and together we grappled for the weapon between us. It did not take long for me to realise he was the stronger, and that my only chance of getting the better of him was to use what skills I had. With both of us clutching the crook for dear life, he pushed me with all of his strength, and suddenly I let go of it, momentarily catching him off balance, and I hit him full in the face. My arsonist grunted and came at me again. I hit him as often as I could, though receiving a few whacks myself. Then it was his turn to come at me, this time swinging the accursed crook again. I backed away saved only by the tent roofing crashing down between us. To hell with this for a game o' soldiers I thought, and staggered out of the burning tent, my own life paramount to fighting this lunatic. Once outside I gulped in fresh air awaiting my antagonist to emerge so that we could start all over again. He didn't.

 Everything seemed to be in state of flux; everywhere there were people dashing here and there. A fireman stopped briefly, to ask if I was all right, before dashing off to tackle the burning marquees, a little further down the park. Another explosion; flames shooting heavenwards: ash slowly raining down like dirty snow, blotting out the sky above us.

 Coughing I made my way back to the distillery, so far untouched by the fire. Outside I made out the figure of Sue, Amanda by her side. A little distance away, Simon was shouting and gesturing to the firemen, as if he knew better on how to deal with the situation. Then, as if he had given up to the inevitable, with a final gesture of despair, turned for the distillery.

 By the time I had reached the building, the two women, now joined by Neil Grant sat forlornly in the main office, with Simon ranting and raving as he paced up and down.

 He saw me give Sue a sympathetic smile as I entered the office. It was all the man needed to vent his spleen on someone, and that someone just happened to be me.

 "What the bloody hell have you got to smile about, you useless moron?" he screeched at me, his eyes blazing hatred. "I hope you don't think I'll pay you after this?"

Now my own anger matched this of my client when I thought of what I would lose in fees and expenses. "You were to pay me for finding Jock Fraser, not to prevent a bloody fire from starting on your own premises, so you can cut that out for a start." I hurled the words across the room at him, and was tempted to follow with my body, but managed to restrain myself.

"That's enough!" Amanda sprung to her feet. "Mr Barns is right. You are obliged to pay him for what he has done."

"And what exactly has he done?" 'Cold eyes' glared at Amanda as he spoke, but the question was directed at me.

Good question I thought, what exactly had I done in the way of finding the old man?

In order to give myself time to construct an answer that would silence this upstart, I changed tack.

"You hired me because you thought I was not capable of finding Jock Fraser before the promotion started, for reasons best known to you. You did so, to keep yourself on the right side of the law, so that in the event that should anything have happened to the old bloke, you could always defend your actions by saying that you had hired a Private Detective; in this case, me. So you need not now go to the police, they are coming to you. So when you are explaining the fire to them, you may also decide to explain why you hired me."

"I think we have more urgent things to attend to, rather than whether you will pay Mr Barns his fee or not, Simon." It was Neil Grant who spoke as he rose to his feet. "I believe we can write off most of the tents and their contents. This includes all the tartan wear and regalia. Whiskies?..." he twisted a hand. "Not so much of a loss there. We are insured for such a calamity, as well as public liability. So far, I have not heard of anyone being injured."

"Except for the guy who started the fire," I said, and watched for Simon MacDonald's reaction.

"Are you trying to say that the fire was started deliberately?" His eyes bore into me, and I knew by his look of sheer disbelief that he had nothing to do with it.

"Millar Mackay!" Amanda roared, " that ..."

"Don't be so hasty Amanda," Sue tried to steady her. "No one in their right mind would want to commit arson on such a scale. Millar

MacKay and his partner might want this Company pretty badly but not at the expense of injuring or killing some innocent people in the process."

"Sue is right," Neil agreed. "Business can be pretty cut throat at times, but never to this degree...at least not in the whisky trade."

When I left they were still debating as what to do best for the restoration of the Company. The promotion that they had worked so hard for, and which in turn they had hoped would see them out of their present financial crises, had been destroyed. But the Company was still viable (enough I hoped, to receive my fee, was my mercenary thought). It was still worth a few millions. Although at present, the fate of old Jock appeared to be of little concern to them, I thought.

I had just stepped outside, when from around the corner came Detective Constable Thomson. He drew up greeting me sourly with, "Oh, it's you again. Do you live here?"

"More likely die." I told him about my encounter with the arsonist, and to the best of my knowledge a faint description of the man, and where he was to be found, or what was left of him.

"You'll have to call at the office, to give a statement,"

By the tone of his voice I knew he was enjoying himself at the prospect of grilling me, under the guise of asking me a 'few questions.' Why, I thought was it always 'a few questions? And if I knew, Bert Thomson well enough, I could well be there for bed and breakfast.

I had just agreed to his demands and he had started indoors when Sue came out.

"I'm sorry I didn't catch up with you sooner. What the hell is happening West? First Gramps then this." Her voice shook as she waved a hand to encompass the burning tents where firemen were still battling with the blaze.

"I don't know Sue, but I still mean to find out, with or without the patronage of good old Simon," I said bitterly.

She stared into my eyes. "Don't worry, West, the Company is still worth millions. I will see that you are paid."

Strangely it was not the money that made me say what I had said, it was something more sinister that worried me. "Never mind, Sue," I said reassuringly, " I'll get to the bottom of it as the man said when he fell down the well."

She chuckled at my joke. "Good, I'll take your word for it."

"Well, there is nothing much you can do here, is there?" I sighed. "Not with this going on all around." I gestured to the burning tents, with thick black smoke wafting towards us.

"You bet there is," she said bitterly. She coughed and put up a hand to her throat. "Simon will have me up half the night, looking into accounts; who has contracted what etc. and I imagine Neil will have me do the same."

The smoke was getting thicker, and I took her arm and guided her back towards the safety of the distillery. "In that case you will need a break. Perhaps we could meet tomorrow sometime, let's say for lunch? I suggested hopefully, and reached for a handkerchief to cover my mouth.

"It would have to be local. I don't think with all that has happened, Simon, or Neil for that matter, will spare me for very long."

"Ok. Pick you up at two. Will that suit?"

"Better make it half past."

I left ,choking in the black smoke but feeling much happier than I thought I would, after my close encounter of the nasty kind.

As I left through the now much guarded front gate in my car, the road seemed to be jam packed with every sort of emergency vehicle, beside those of the curious kind, and it took me quite a time to wind my way through those parked on the road, and in some places the grass verges.

Being somewhat cautious as regards my no claim insurance bonus, I slid Geraldine in between two cars parked in the opposite direction from one another, and edged my way through, when I saw away to my left a Toyota Pick- up, being driven at high speed away from the perimeter fence. At first I thought it might be a news reporter hurrying back before his particular paper was put to bed as they say, but somehow my gut feeling told me otherwise. Kicking Geraldine into third, I prepared to follow the speeding car.

It took me some time before I was anywhere near keeping the black Toyota in sight with Geraldine puffing and panting in her own mechanical way. At last I got close enough to memorise the registration number before the Pick-up began to slow and the driver waved me on. "Shit," I said aloud, and it had indeed hit the fan, for I was fast approaching the crossroads, and the sign which read

Haddington one way, Bolton the other.

Now that I was ahead of the vehicle I did not know which direction to take. If I guessed wrongly and he went in the opposite direction from which I had taken, then I would undoubtedly lose him. Which way, Geraldine? Whether it was because the road sloped downwards that my car chose this way or not, that I found myself heading towards Haddington, and much to my delight the Pick-up had done the same.

However my troubles were not yet over. Now being in front of the Toyota I did not know which way it was headed, and I would have to get behind it once more to find out where.

At the bottom of the hill there was a secondary road leading away to the left, I took it and gradually slowed down and watched in my rear mirror as the Pick-up sped past.

Executing a three-point turn which would have instantly failed me in my driving test, I started after the speeding vehicle.

Thankfully my quarry had halted at the traffic lights and I was able to catch up and follow him as he took off up one of Haddington's one-way streets. However, the danger was, should he spot me behind him, he would know that having taken off down the secondary road, I was in fact following him. I pulled back a little and let him draw ahead. Now we were on the old A1 road, and I followed at a discreet distance until he took the exit on to the by-pass to Edinburgh.

The Toyota did not leave any of the slip roads all the way to the city. It had been easy following him on the by-pass as I could keep several cars behind him without him being aware of me, or so I hoped, but now in the outskirts of the city it was a different matter.

It took almost an hour before the Pick-up reached its destination; a house in the New Town. The driver, a strongly built man in his late thirties got out and I was glad he had not spotted me, for had he done so he would probably put me into the ground like a tent peg. I swallowed hard at the thought and waited while he let himself into the house.

Now it was up to Fenton I decided when I phoned and gave him the registration number of the Toyota Pick-up, and the address of the house, to find out where it would lead, if indeed anywhere. Of course this was without the illustrious, Inspector Thomson knowing about it.

Sue looked at the posh surrounds of the restaurant I had taken her to. "You cannot afford this West," she said, the alarm clear in his voice.

I gave a shrug, "I can always put it on expenses," I said deadpan, "that's providing my client has anything left to pay me with."

"The Company, as I said before is not so hard up."

"What about the fire?"

"The insurance will cover our losses."

"I didn't mean that Sue. The fire was started deliberately."

"Not one of us would do such an evil thing." Sue stared at me, daring me to contradict her.

"What about Millar Mackay? He had the most to gain."

"It's a distillery Company we're talking about, West, not the Mafia." Sue sat back to let the waiter place the main course in front of her.

I lifted my fork to mine; fish and chips suited me, as I had better play it safe financially just in case the good firm of MacDonald Fraser came up short, and I didn't mean 'short' as in whisky.

"Besides the fire, how well did the promotion do?" The fish was excellent, and I took another bite as I awaited Sue's answer.

"Neil did his best with the overseas clients, but most wanted to deal with old Jock, 'the boss' himself." She looked at me through her brows. "You still think Gramps is dead, don't you? And that Ewen Cameron has something to do with it."

"A lot to do with it. He is in the right place to move the treasure and reap the glory for himself. And," I emphasised, "he has all the time in the world to do it."

"I don't know any of Ewen's family, and when I was with you, I met Craig for the first time. Poor boy what will he think if his uncle get's locked up?"

The conversation was turning sour. I had hoped to cheer this girl up, but I could see the whole affair had deeply disturbed her. "Desserts are very good here,"

"I think I will pass. Just coffee for me please, but you have one, you deserve it." She did her best to smile.

Thinking of the savings, I said, "Coffee will be just fine for me too."

Wednesday evening found me sitting in my car in a gutted dirt road running a little distance away from the MacDonald mansion. The case had become that little bit too complicated for my liking. First, there was a missing man to be found. Secondly, was his disappearance indeed connected to Prince Charles Edward Stuart's gold? Thirdly, had all this, or any of it anything to do with the fire at the distillery?

Suddenly it had come to me like the result of a curry from the night before. What if in fact the old man was still alive? If so, could he have been behind the attempt to burn down his own distillery? And if so what would he gain?

According to Sue, the promotion had been adequately covered by the insurance, and no damage had been done to the distillery itself. This being the case, my theory of Ewen Cameron, being responsible for old Jock's death had gone up in flames with the promotion tents, as had my suspicions of Millar Mackay being involved.

I had had these thoughts earlier, over a glass of much needed MacDonald Fraser whisky as I listened to my favourite record; ABBA singing 'Money Money Money' Should my theory of the old man being alive prove correct, where was he hiding? It had to be local I should think, or then again maybe not. He could have someone inside the Company or the 'family' even, carrying out his orders. I snapped my fingers, not to the music but at the notion I had cracked it. Where better to hide than in his old friend's Archie's house, which Sue had told me, had remained empty since the old man's passing.

So here I was sitting in my car a little way from the main driveway of the big grey mansion house of the late Archie MacDonald, founder of the entire Company.

"It won't get much darker than this at this time of year," I said to my passenger; or accomplice really.

"So you think we might get in by the back way?" the diminutive figure of Harry Muir, asked, beside me.

Fenton had put the wee man away for safe cracking a few years back, and to my knowledge Harry had almost - I say almost - gone straight since then. Now here I was asking him to break the law, who, if caught would serve an even longer custodial sentence, probably with me as his cellmate.

"It's up to you," I said clearing my throat, but not my mind of what I was actually about to do, "you're the expert."

We both got out of the car, and keeping bushes and anything else that would afford us cover, eventually reached the side of the driveway.

"No burglar alarm," Harry whispered to me. "Maybe it's been stolen," he added with a chuckle.

I looked up to where he was staring towards the roof.

"What do you think; front door or back?" I asked, looking quickly around me like some bird on the look-out for sudden predators.

"Let's try the back. Here at the front there is always the chance of being seen from the road by the odd passing vehicle."

I complied and we started to work our way round to the rear of the building.

"This place must have cost a fortune," Harry surmised letting out a low whistle. "It much be bung-fu inside."

"You mind and leave 'the bung' where it is," I warned my accomplice.

"Not even a wee 'bung'," Harry smiled up at me in the semi darkness.

"No. I don't want anyone to know that someone has broken in. Understand Harry?"

"You're the boss," he sighed in resignation.

There were French doors midways along the back wall. Harry made for them and tried the door handle. "No trouble getting in here boss, if you want."

I did want. I took a look up and along the length of the building. The house seemed deserted, and nowhere was there even a glimmer of light from any of the rooms.

It seemed only seconds before Harry had the door open and we were inside. I shone my pencil torch around the room where we stood. It was a sun lounge, should 'sun' be the appropriate word. A colourful settee stood facing into the large garden, where a well trimmed lawn was bordered by various species of plants and flowers, proving, though the house was unoccupied that the grounds were still being well maintained.

I opened the door, and peered down the dark corridor. "I'll try down here. You stay here and keep watch," I ordered, and started forward.

Halfway down the corridor, a room to my right contained a single bed, set of drawers and a leather armchair. I moved on. The corridor was brighter now as I drew closer to the front of the house and its huge bay windows. Here to my left was a large well equipped kitchen. I took a few steps inside and shone my torch around, carefully keeping its beam well below window level. I moved to the work bench, and without thinking, felt the side of the electric kettle. I gasped, it was warm, and as I swung round, my torch lit up two cups in the sink. Did one belong to old Jock? Either that or there were still two people in the house, or they had just left.

My problem was, should I continue my search for evidence of old Jock being here? Or should I just leave? Quit while ahead. But I wasn't ahead, I had not gained anything by breaking into this house, and would not do so until I had explored the entire premises.

For a brief moment as I once again stood in the corridor, I hoped Harry would signal that someone was coming up the driveway, and give me an excuse not to explore further. He did not, and with a heavy, but, I hoped silent sigh, made for the stairway leading to what I believed to be the upstairs bedroom.

As I took my first tentative step on the stair, I could not imagine what I would say should a light suddenly switch on at the head of the stairs and leave me staring up at them with my mouth open like a goldfish in a bowl. It was entirely possible that whoever was up there was here legitimately, which I certainly was not. Then what was I to do, or say? Perhaps goodbye would be a suitable answer as I took to my heels.

Although to me my steps were light on the long stairs, every creak was like the sound of trees in a gale. Or was it my own creaking limbs? I kept my eyes on the landing above, waiting that moment when the light went on. Still, all remained silent, except for the ticking of a clock in the hall below, and my knocking knees.

After each cautious step, I at last reached the top landing. Here there were three doors facing me, with another to my left. I decided to try this one first as it was the nearest. Holding my breath I turned the door handle and gently pushed the door open. It was too dark to see into the room, despite the last of the evening's light filtering through the one and only window. I took a step inside, and saw that it was a bedroom, this one much larger than the one I had discovered in the corridor downstairs. The double bed appeared neat and tidy, and I had the feeling that it had not been used for quite some time. As I stepped further into the room, a photograph on the bedside table took my attention. It was the last I remember seeing, before the back of my head exploded in bright lights, then the lights went out and I felt myself falling.

It must be December because I was shivering. Someone was holding me in a sitting position, asking if I was all right and I heard myself answer that it was a stupid question to ask, as I always felt all right with a thumping headache and bump on my head, the size of which would qualify me as a 'Munroe.'

I slowly turned my head round and stared into the anxious face of Harry Muir and wondered why he was here. "Hello Harry, have they let you out again," I muttered through a thick veil covering my eyes.

"I think I should get you home mister ex-polis man," I heard him say from afar.

I leaned on his arm and shakily struggled to my feet. "What has happened, Harry?" Now it was slowly coming back to me why we were here.

Harry sat me down on the edge of the bed. "I think someone decided to use your head as a baseball, and clouted you one with their bat, who ever, they were." At my puzzled look he went on. "Two of them, a man and a woman. I only glimpsed them as they rushed down the stairs. I saw them take off in a car from this window when I came to see what had happened to you."

"Thanks Harry." I changed my mind about standing up again as the room began to swim around me. "Did you catch the colour of the car by any chance? They must have parked it out of sight in one of the double garages, that's why we thought the house was empty."

"Nope. They were out of the drive as if they were a late entry in the Belgium Grand Prix."

At last as my head began to clear I got up. "Let's see what they were up to, that they didn't want anyone to know about."

With Harry's help I searched the other room on the top landing where I thought my attacker must have come from. It was another bedroom. This time the bed was unmade, and the clothes looked as if they had been hastily flung aside, and a pillow lay on the floor.

"Now you know what they have been up to," Harry said looking at the unmade bed.

I turned from the door. "Yes, Harry but who, that is the question? I don't think they were a couple of squatters who had found the house unoccupied."

"You're right there, Mister West Barns. I think you're definitely right there. Now let's get you home before you fall down again."

Next day despite my headache, I left for my office, the cheerful sound of laughter from one of the offices further down the corridor having me cringe at the sound. The same as had some irate lady motorist honking her horn at me for pulling away from the traffic lights too slowly and having her running late for her accident. I had just got in to my office, when the phone rang. With my head still thumping, I dreaded to hear the sound of my favourite dog lover, old Mrs MacKenzie on the other end. Instead it was Fenton.

"Hello there, old buddy. How's it going?" he asked in his usual cheerful voice.

"If you mean my head, it's going round and round," and I answered his inquiry as to why.

There was a moments silence on the other end, until finally he said. "I don't know what you've got yourself into, brother of mine, but if that address in Edinburgh you had me check out has anything to do with it, you've got yourself involved with some very nasty characters, to say the least."

I told him he must understand my position, but I would give him as much information as ethically possible. He agreed, and after exchanging a few pleasantries, I put the phone down.

I decided I needed something stronger for my headache, so I stepped down to the printer's office at the end of the corridor.

"Hello! No time, no see, as the old blind sailor said," Maggie the receptionist greeted me warmly.

"No, I was away having my bumps read," I pointed to my head.

"Too slow at getting your trousers on," she laughed.

"If only," I answered. "No, I tripped over old Mrs MacKenzie's dog," I answered, as earlier I had asked them for a quote to have some flyers printed.

"So you won't need any flyers done?" Her question was rhetorical, and she laughed.

"No, but I could do with an aspirin or something stronger for this headache."

"Would a dog powder help?" Maggie's eyes gleamed as she rose.

Clearly I had made her day.

"No, but you can have me put down if you like."

"Could do. I've always been kind to dumb animals."

I finished the quip for her, "And I sure am dumb."

After a time Maggie's cracks matched the one in my head, so after a welcome cup of coffee and two co-codamol tablets later, I returned to my office.

When next the phone rang it was to further add to my headache, it was Bert Thomson asking me..or to be more precise, telling me to meet him in his office at the station that morning. So with a heavy heart and a head to match, I set out for the big city.

Bert's welcome was about as warm as a Polar Bears arse on an iceberg.

I sat down across from him at his desk, and with not so much as a 'thank you for calling' or 'can I get you something to drink', he got straight to the point, and I wondered how Fenton could cope with such an unpleasant character as this. Most officers would have been pleased to have a witness to the crimes they were investigating, but Thomson was the opposite. Perhaps Fenton showed him up too much, but I guessed he would not be the only one to have done so.

"So, you didn't get a good look at this guy you were fighting with in the tent?"

"No. To all intent and purposes, I was too busy defending myself," I replied as civilly as I could, at the same time wondering if he had realised I had made a pun.

"If I were to show you some mug shots would it help?"

"A mug of coffee maybe and a shot of whisky maybe, but no." I felt a bit daft at having said this, but, I thought if I could annoy him sufficiently, he might let me go, just for the sake of not having to listen to my daft jokes.

"Oh, very nice, West. It's not difficult to see where your brother gets it from. Now, can I ask you again, do you think you could pick him out in a mug shot?"

Thomson was getting angrier now and it was my own fault. But somehow this moron always managed to annoy me, and my headache was not getting any better.

"As I said, I couldn't get a good look at him through the smoke and having to ward off his blows half the time."

"Mm." Thomson scribbled something in his note book and I

didn't think it was 'mm'.

"A lot of help you've been. A right waste of time getting you down here, Barns. Are you sure there is nothing else that could help with our inquiries?"

I asked myself what I thought Fenton would do if he were in my position. Would he tell the moron here about the guy in the Toyota Pick-up? I decided that he would, so I told him, as I knew that it was not breaking client confidentiality.

When I had finished, Thomson did not look much like the confident sod he had been a few moments before. "You are sure of this?" He swallowed. "Do you know what you are into?"

I stood up. "What you are into Braveheart, I'm only the messenger boy." I smiled down at him. "Is it, you can't deal with the East Coast Mafia?" I laughed. "The Port Seton branch, rowing over to Kuwait to sell cans of oil at knock down prices, too much for you?"

He looked up at me unable to digest my little, but stupid joke.

"You must be absolutely certain of what you have seen before we go anywhere near that address."

"Wrong again," I said, tapping the desk with the point of my finger. "You must be absolutely certain. All I can tell you, is, what I saw. Perhaps the Pick-up was there on some legitimate, business, I don't know. It's for you to find out. So, if there is nothing else I can do for you, I wish you a very good day."

I left the office with much relief, for I was sure that when I arrived, Thomson's intentions were to keep me there with 'just a few more questions' and I would have to send out for bacon rolls before he let me go.

Now I was not so sure what this was all about. It had started with a missing man, that his Company did not want the police to know about; a treasure he might have found and died for around Loch Arkaig; promotion tents burned down by the local Mob, my being hit on the napper for discovering a love nest. And to top it all, I still had not found old Mrs MacKenzie's dog! What a bloody day!

It had come to me over the weekend, in between meeting Sue and lying awake at night… unfortunately alone. It would be a dangerous thing to do, and should it fail I could end up walking on the bottom of the River Forth wearing a pair of cement trainers.

I had met Millar MacKay, but not his partner; this is why I decided to take the chance of phoning their Company that Monday morning.

"Could I speak to Mr Millar MacKay, please." I asked as politely as possible, with my heart beating at twice its normal rate. I had my excuse ready should it be he who answered; instead, I heard.

"I am sorry, Mr Mackay is away on business and will not be back until Thursday at the earliest," was the crisp reply from the other end of the phone.

"Very well. Then is it possible to speak to Mr Grey. It is quite urgent."

"Hold on and I will ask him. Who shall I say is calling?"

I had my name all ready for such a question. "Andrew Kemp," I replied, just as politely as before, with my heart still beating as fast as before. I looked at the phone in my hand, as if it could give me the right advice. Perhaps this was not a good idea after all.

Too late, I heard the same crisp voice on the other end. "Hello, Mr Kemp, Mr Grey could see you this afternoon at 2pm, if this would suit you?"

"Splendid. 2pm will suit me just fine. And I thank you for your help." My fumbling with the phone as I put it back in its cradle was purely the result of my shaking hand.

Now I had three nerve racking hours to wait.

It was quite difficult to find a parking space anywhere near the Leith Docks. Eventually I found a parking space some distance away from the office I intended to visit, so there was no chance of anyone connecting me with my visit with Mr Grey.

By the sound of her voice, it was the same receptionist who greeted me as the one who had spoken to me on the phone. She was much older than I had imagined: I hated to think what impression she had of me.

"Please take a seat Mr Kemp, Mr Grey will see you shortly." She offered me what I thought, was one of her routine smiles.

I conveyed my thanks, and sat myself down on a plush leather chair by the wall. I looked around at the smart modern office with its abstract pictures and cut glass ornaments, and was not quite sure what they intended to represent.

I lifted a magazine, surprisingly not out of date, unlike the ones in dental and doctors' surgeries announcing the sinking of the Titanic or the latest news on the Battle of the Somme.

"Mr Grey will see you now, sir." The receptionist broke my interest. "Up the stairs, first door to your left." She had risen to point the way.

I thanked her and putting down my magazine I started for the stairs, my stomach and my mind churning at what I was about to do.

Grey, was a man in his mid forties, of medium build and a look which said 'I hope this visit is going to be financially rewarding, and not wasting my time.'

I shook his hand and took the proffered seat in front of his desk.

"Well, Mr Kemp, what can I do for you?"

Now that I was here, I was not quite sure myself, or of myself. I cleared my throat and took on what I hoped was a convincing pose of a gangster – stroke - criminal who was completely sure of what he was about.

"The Boss has decided he wants the cash for the job by tomorrow."

Now I waited; should Grey ask what boss, I was undone.

Instead, much to my relief he spread out his hands in a gesture of incredulity. "The agreement was for Friday of next week." His voice had risen an octave or two.

My heart beating faster by the second at this unexpected admission of acknowledging of who my 'Boss' was, I gave a shrug of indifference. "The Boss says have the money ready tomorrow, and I have to tell you where to meet." I gave him a cold stare, which I hoped would negate any suspicion he may have had should the meeting place have been previously decided.

His hand went to the phone. "Perhaps I should speak to your Boss, this was not the agreement."

I leaned across the desk, and placed my hand none too gently on his. "The Boss would not like that. No calls you understand, especially when he has made his mind up, and sent me to make up yours."

It was the first time Mr Jack Grey looked flustered. "Tomorrow is impossible." He quickly drew his hand away from under mine.

I sat back in my chair and looked him squarely in the eye. "The Boss does not understand the word impossible, Mr Grey."

For a moment he sat there, toying with a letter opener. "I could have the cash together by Wednesday, if this would suit your boss?"

I tried not to show my relief. So it was this man who had ordered the fire at the distillery, perhaps his partner, Millar MacKay also.

I studied my hands in my lap for a time in pretence of contemplating a decision, and I decided not to push my luck too far. I sighed. "The Boss did say tomorrow, and he is not a man to be contradicted. However, I will take it upon myself to agree to your suggestion."

He watched me rise from my chair, as I said, "the arrangements for receiving the money are slightly different from what they were originally." I threw a sketch of a map I had drawn, down on his desk. "This will be the new meeting place. Do you know it?"

Grey drew the map towards him, and studied it for a moment. "Why so far away as East Lothian ? Our agreement was here in Edinburgh."

"If the Boss chooses to change the location, he must have a good reason. He didn't get where he is today by being careless. Ok?"

Grey gave a nod of resignation. "Midnight, at Longniddry Bents." He stood up. Hope to see you there, Mr Kemp."

"I hope so too," I said, and wished him a good day.

My next interview of the day, was at Fettes with Detective Constable Thomson, and I sincerely hoped he was on duty. He was.

I outlined my earlier conversation with Jack Grey and my plan to trap him at Longniddry. He could of course veto the whole idea, but if he did it would be out of sheer animosity, directed either at me or my brother, or both.

"Why did you chose that particular spot?" he asked.

Thomson had done a bad job of disguising his enthusiasm, so I knew I had him hooked. I could see he had promotion written all over his face, and probably other places too, that I couldn't see.

"There is only one way in and out. At that time of night there will only be the odd lovers in their cars. These could be your cars if you get there early enough."

"And what if there are others? We have to think of public safety?"

"I don't think it will end in a gunfight, Longniddry's not Chicago, or the Pans," I said, the latter tongue in cheek.

Thomson sat staring at a current file on his desk, probably one on Jack The Ripper.

"What if your Mr Grey doesn't turn up, and in the meantime he has contacted, Simonson, who has found out that it was not one of his men who has made these arrangements? Simonson, is no fool you know. That's why he is where he is today."

"Agreed. If Grey has done as you say and got in touch with Simonson, that man will want to know who this traitor is, and if it is not one of his own men, how he came to know about the deal in the first place."

Thomson stared at the file on his desk. "It's a bit far-fetched, Barns." His eyes lifted to mine.

"It's a chance worth taking. If you catch those who were concerned with burning down the MacDonald Fraser, promotion, you will be a hero. More so, if Simonson himself turns up, even if it is out of curiosity as to who this person is who is trying to do him out of his money."

I watched Thomson deliberate over what I had said. If he was the person to put Simonson away, it would mean certain promotion. To get one up on his fellow colleagues, especially my brother was clearly going through his mind.

Thomson cleared his throat. "I will have to run it by my superiors. If they give it the go-ahead I will make the arrangements and get back to you. Wednesday, should give me enough time. OK?"

Fine, I thought, if this looked anywhere like succeeding there would be more senior officers there than you could poke a stick at, and all hoping to share in the credit of nabbing Simonson in the act.

As I got to my feet to leave, suddenly Thomson asked. "Why are you doing this Barns? I could see the sense in your coming to your brother with this idea of yours, but why me, of all people?"

"It's my clients who are suffering as the result of the fire, Thomson, and men like Simonson are better off the street. Don't you think so? I gave him my warmest smile. "Besides, my brother is away up in Inverness." I winked at him and left.

By 11pm that Wednesday, the beach and surrounding area at Longniddry Bents was almost deserted. A few cars that remained were mostly unmarked police cars.

Sitting in my own car on Gosford Road, I waited patiently for the hour of midnight to approach. Now I wished I had not got myself involved in this side of the business. What I had told Thomson about my wanting justice for my client was not strictly true, and if I was to be honest with myself it was more to do with my trying to impress a certain young lady in their employ. Somehow in my mind

I was hoping our acquaintanceship would continue after this case was closed. It was time I settled down, and I knew it could work between us.

I drummed my fingers on the steering wheel, and breathed as easily as I could in an attempt to remain calm. Should things go wrong, not only would I be in deep shit with Thomson, but should Simonson find out that it was me who was behind this little charade, I would be in even greater shit…a sewerage works deep, I should think.

I was in two minds as regards my wishing it was midnight. One, that it couldn't come fast enough, another that it wouldn't come at all. Then, although I had thought my watch had stopped it was time to be on the move.

I drove the car through the park gate and onto the path beyond. A short distance away the moon shone on the steel grey waters of the Forth, and in the distance the twinkling lights of Kirkcaldy across the river.

I drove onto a grass verge and waited. Grey had said his car was a white BMW. So far there was none there. Facing towards Port Seton there was only one other car, parked where it overlooked the Forth. I hoped it contained police and not any of Simonson's men.

I looked nervously around me. Should Simonson be aware of the meeting, he would surely have been here by now, waiting for me the 'traitor' or of some unknown 'chancer' to rob him of his cash. Then again would he? Could he have men waiting some distance away from the Bents, waiting for Grey and me to meet?

As I was mulling this over in my mind, a car with its lights switched off came through the gate and made towards me, and as it drew closer I saw that it was a white BMW. I waited until it had pulled up a little way from where I sat, and taking a long deep breath I got out, and walked towards it.

Halfway there the door opened and Grey got out. "Kemp," he said and held up the black case he was carrying.

I felt my knees tremble as I drew nearer, waiting anxiously for the comforting sound of a police siren; there was none.

Shit, I thought, has Thomson buggered it up? Has he got the time wrong? Or has his superiors had second thoughts?

I was at the car now and Grey held out the case to me. "Do you wish to count it, Mr Kemp? I am sure your boss would want you to do so."

There was something in the mocking way he had said it that instantly startled me. He appeared to be pretty cocksure of himself as he took a step towards me. God, I thought, and looked for his free hand sliding under his jacket. Is he going to shoot me? Where the hell was Thomson's mob?

Suddenly, and before I realised what had happened, the rear door of the BMW opened and two men got out.

"Mr Kemp?" one said.

I took a hasty step back. I didn't like the look of these Blues Brothers. Who were they? Were they Simonson's men? Or were these two hard men Grey had recruited solely for the evening?

The one nearest took a run at me and I backed away, ready to run for my car, though I had little hope even should I reach it, of throwing myself in, turning on the ignition and getting the hell out of here. Where the hell were Thomson and his gang? Probably giving out parking tickets somewhere.

The first thug was now within striking distance; striking distance of me that was. He lashed out and I dodged the cement fist, punched him in the midriff and backed off as his pal, came at me from the side. I heard a laugh from Grey who I supposed was enjoying watching the man he believed had tried to swindle him, getting a 'right dooin'.

It was then I heard the sound of a siren; at least I hoped it was a siren and not the ringing in my ears from a blow from the second Blues brother.

They had me cornered now against the bonnet of my car and I was warding off the blows, but none too successfully. I felt my teeth introducing themselves to one another and I felt blood in my mouth. If I was to go down, a severe kicking would undoubtedly follow. Now I wished I had stuck to just looking for old Fraser, or even for that matter old Mrs MacKenzie's dog.

Fortunately my assertion that it was a siren I had heard proved correct, and out of the corner of my eye (the one they had not hit) I saw the interior light of a parked car go on, the door open and two bodies running towards me, at the same time as the place appeared to teem with blue uniforms. The cavalry had arrived!

"Where the hell have you been?"I shouted at Thomson as he supervised the arrest of my two assailants.

"We had to wait until they made their move," he said as if was normal police procedure.

"Wait!" I shouted. "Wait until they half killed me and you had them on an attempted murder charge! Moron!"

Thomson's face lit up, and he beamed at me. "I got them didn't I?"

My teeth ached as I stormed at him. "You got them! What was I doing while you got them, singing Hello! Hello! Nice to see you?"

"Simonson is not here sir." A uniform informed Thomson.

Thomson looked at me and gave a shrug. "Can't win them all, but we do have enough on this lot to make a case. Of course, we'll need you to testify, Barns."

I shook my head. "Not against Simonson, you're on your own there, boy."

"Simonson will wriggle out of it as usual. He'll deny any knowledge of what happened here, and any involvement with Grey."

"Unless, Grey involves Simonson," I suggested.

"Can't see him doing that, he's as afraid of that man as you are."

Thomson turned away, and now I really wished I had not got myself involved.

CHAPTER THREE

I waited a couple of days before I drove to the distillery. My jaw had returned to its normal position, and my teeth seemed to be all right, although I thought my gums would have to come out. The swelling around my eye had gone down, and the cut above my eye was covered by a plaster.

Amanda MacDonald did her best to hide her shock when she saw me through the glass partition of the main office. "Started a new war have you?" she asked giving me an almost sympathetic smile.

"Something like that."

Just then Simon came in, followed by Sue. Now at last I would receive some genuine sympathy, from Sue that is.

"You should see the other guy," I said before he had time to comment on my appearance.

"West! What on earth has happened to you?" Sue came to me and looked up sadly into my eyes. Now it seemed to be all worthwhile.

Briefly…well not too briefly I told them of my little episode with Jack Grey and co.

"So it was Millar MacKay and his partner who tried to ruin us," Simon said angrily. "I should have known. He always has had his eye on this business."

I held up my hand. "Grey, yes, but the police, and also for my part, are not quite sure that Millar MacKay was involved."

"Why did you do it, West, you were not hired to risk your life as you did?" Sue took my hand, and I felt myself as faint as I had when the Blues Brothers attacked me.

"Nor is he paid to do so. His remit was to find old Jock," Simon snarled, as he sat down at his desk.

"Oh! You beast Simon! West went out of his way to find out who sabotaged the promotion as you were his client. The least you can do, is thank him," Sue stormed at her employer.

Good on you Sue, I thought, but never mind the thanks, just sign the cheque Simon.

"Oh, it's West now is it" Simon sneered, and I wished he had been one of the Blues Brothers.

Just then Neil Grant came in. He looked at me and turned up a lip.

"Sue being belting you up again, West?" he cackled, and threw a sheaf of papers down on Simon's desk.

Sue drew her hand away, and made a face at my new joker.

"I need you, Sue, for those accounts. Something doesn't add up." He stood waiting as if expecting Sue to precede him out of the office.

"Have a heart, Neil, I've been here since six this morning," she exclaimed, giving him what I thought would be one of her most uncharitable looks, "and I have not had lunch yet."

"Ok, grab a bite in the cafeteria. Try and be back as quickly as possible."

"All right if I keep you company? I'm a bit peckish myself," I asked the angry girl.

"That would be nice. I need a break away from the maddening crowd," she threw over her shoulder as she took my hand escorted me out of the office.

"I can see now how they treat you Sue. Was it like that when your Gramps was around?" I asked as I sipped my coffee.

"Only when he loaned me to them if they were especially busy. He didn't really know how they all treated me, and I didn't want to speak behind their backs, or worry the old guy." She gave a sigh. "I wonder where the old soul is now? I think you may be right, West, in your assumption that Gramps is dead, or he would have been at the promotion."

"Should he still be alive, he will be returning to a hell of a mess." I put my partially eaten sandwich down on my plate. "That's if he can offer a valid reason for his absence."

"Simon will lose no time in putting up the business for sale if Gramps is dead. He will become sole owner."

"Won't that take a little time? It'll depend on the old boy's Will."

Sue nodded. "Sure, but there are ways of getting round this..if you have the money...which Simon will have. I don't fancy working solely for him, or for that matter Neil. That boy's too power hungry. Although I must say, he is..." she looked at me, "was Gramps choice over Simon to run the business successfully. Thankfully Simon however reluctantly, acknowledged this, if only for the businesses sake, and should Neil be the means of making him richer, so much the better, as it would mean more money in his pocket when it came to selling the Company."

As Sue bit into her sandwich, I said. "Will you be out of a job? I mean Simon is pretty nasty to you right now."

"I couldn't be much worse off under new management, should Simon keep me on 'till then."

"I wish I could offer you alternative employment, but I'm toiling as it is."

Sue gave me a broad smile. "With living in benefits, I bet?"

If only, I thought, but to make this possible I would have to find the same number of dogs in the Seafield Dogs Home, each week to make ends meet. And I didn't mean dog ends either."

It was Sue's mentioning that Simon would become sole owner of the Company should old Jock no longer be alive, that had me thinking that perhaps the answer lay in the old man's safe, so, once again having solicited the help of my assistant criminal I heard him say, "Are you thinking of taking this up as a career, Mr Barns?" Harry asked, as we sat in my car on a side road a little away from the Fraser residence.

This was to be my second break-in, in less than two weeks, so Harry had cause to ask.

"Compared to you Harry, I'm still on Y.T.S."

I gave my watch a quick glance and sat back. "We might as well get started, it's not going to get any darker."

Harry put his hand on the door handle, and drew me a look, which had 'save me from amateurs like you' written all over it. "You don't know whether this safe is a key or combination job?"

"No. I was only ever in the lounge that one time I was here."

"Could you not have made some excuse to visit again, to make sure where the bloody hell it is?" Harry let out a long sigh of frustration. "There's no guarantee it will be in his study. It might be hidden, unless it has a notice hanging from it saying, here I am." He sighed again as if having resigned himself to another prison stretch. "Well let's get to it, copper." Harry opened the car door and I did the same on my side.

As fortune would have it, the conservatory at the rear of the building was not new; quite old in fact, and strangely out of place in a house of this stature. Harry set to work and had the door open before I had time to look around the walled garden, or pick any of the lovely flowers.

"Piece of cake," he smirked at me.

"No thank you, I ate before I started."

"Wise guy." He curled a lip and pushed open the door. "I hope you're wearing gloves, copper."

"Of course, where do you think I learned my trade?" I pushed him gently into the house.

After a little searching, we found old Jock's study down a corridor, and a little away from the lounge where I had first met 'happy families.' Fortunately luck was still on our side for the safe was an old type, which stood on the floor, instead, as I had expected it to be a combination wall safe.

Harry got quickly to work. "Won't be too hard to crack this one. With all his dough this is all he can afford, miserable old git. Serves him right if he gets taken."

"Just open the dammed thing, Harry, and let me be the judge of that."

"Hope you're the only judge I see, over this." Harry mumbled a few choice words under his breath and opened his box of tricks, and set to work.

While the master was at work I quietly took a look around the house, amazed by such opulence. If this house was anything to judge by, the Company of MacDonald Fraser was nothing close to being on the skids. A quick peek upstairs revealed nothing out of the ordinary, such as no dead 'Gramps' or anything, and I glanced up the driveway from the lounge where I had first seen Sue arrive in her little car, before returning to old Jock's study.

It seemed an eternity, and my eyes were beginning to ache from watching for anything coming up the driveway, before I heard Harry give a muffled cry to attract my attention.

"It's all yours copper." Harry had a smug look on his face as if justly proud of his trade.

"You keep an eye on the front driveway, let me know if you see anything."

Harry nodded, and I added, "Remember Harry, no one has to know that anyone has been here, so keep your hands in your pockets. Ok?"

"Would I do such a thing, Mr Barns?"

"I'll leave that question unanswered for the moment. So get going."

I turned and made my way to the study. If my heart had been pounding faster at being in someone else's property, it was now pounding even faster at the prospect of what I might find in the safe, for I was sure it was in there that I would find all the answers that would solve my case.

I reached the study and kneeled down in front of the open safe with Harry's key still in the lock. I don't mind admitting that my hands shook as I lifted out the first bundle of papers.

I laid my pencil torch down on old Jock's desk, and sat down. A brief scan through them told me it was the old man's, Last Will and Testament. I decided to examine them closer and the hairs on the back of my neck stood rigidly to attention as I did so.

Still stunned by what I had read, I swivelled round on the black leather chair, kneeled down and replaced the papers back in the safe.

It was then that a brown envelope at the back caught my attention and I lifted it out and sat back down on the chair.

I do not know how long I sat there reading what that envelope contained. In some ways I wished I had not. I swivelled back round and sat for a moment staring into the black metal box, unable to believe what I had just read. Now everything was falling into place.

It was as I sat there, time forgotten, that I heard the faint sound of a car and Harry's footsteps running down the corridor towards the study.

"Car coming, we better hop it!" Harry's face was ghostly in the pencil beam of my torch, and then it was gone as he started back to where we had made our illegal entrance.

I quickly switched off the torch as the front door opened. Shit I thought, there was no time for me to get away. Very near to panic, I tried to shove the documents back into the brown envelope only to find in my haste that some sheets had caught on the side.

Footsteps in the corridor, coming this way. In the darkness I tried again as I ducked down beside the safe and tossed the envelope inside, and as calmly as possible closed the door, and locked it, thrusting the key into my pocket.

The footsteps were almost at the study door. There was no way out without being seen. I ducked under the desk, and stopped the chair from moving.

Holding my breath I sat hunched there like a twenty seven year old foetus. The light went on, and as I saw a pair of trousers pass by, and I concluded that my visitor was male.

Now it was inevitable that this pair of trousers was going to sit down at the desk, and if so, if he failed to see me, he would not when he kicked me in my penalty area.

I thought out what I would say when he caught me under the desk. Something such as, 'Just looking for my contacts lens, nice weather for this time of year, or 'after all I am working under cover.'

However, God and the taxman was on my side for once, trousers stepped to the far wall and lifted a file from the bookcase and although his back was towards me I could not fail to recognise the figure as that of none other than, Neil Grant. He turned, and I held my breath; this time there was no doubt that he would sit down at the desk. It was then I heard the continuous blast of a motor horn, and Neil turned quickly and left the study.

I rose as silently and as quickly as my cramped legs would allow, and with a final glance down the corridor took off after my accomplice.

Harry was sitting in my car when I wrenched the door open.

"Thanks, Harry," I puffed at him, not yet having fully recovered my breath or my nerves.

"I thought you'd be in a spot of bother, if whoever it was came into the study, so I nipped out and did my little trick with his car's horn; seemed to work," Harry chuckled. "Did you get what you were after?"

I nodded and started up the car. "And more, Harry, and more."

The following day found me back in my office, staring at a blank wall with an expression to match. What did I really want to do in life? Those had also been my thoughts when pensioned out of the Force. Starting up this P.I. business had been a last resort.

Catching unfaithful husbands, and come to think of it wives, was not the most exciting way of earning a crust, but at least it was comparatively safe, unless you were caught by an irate husband, or even worse a wife, then you were in the hundred metres sprint business instead.

This case was entirely different. One bump on the head, a fight with a 'heidbanger' then two 'hard men,' from the local Mafia, was not my kind of business either. I sighed and got up. I still had a divorce case, and the weekly rent to contend with. However, a phone call that evening was to change all that, yet again.

It must have been close on midnight when my mobile rang, just as I was about to get my head down and do some uninterrupted snoring. I picked it up to hear the excited voice of young Craig on the other end.

"West, is that you?"

"Sure is," I yawned. "What can I do for you at this time of night? You should be in bed as all good schoolboys should be."

He brushed my banter aside. "West, I have found it! I have found the cave!"

The last time someone had 'found it' they had gone missing.

"Are you sure, Craig?" I hoped I did not sound too condescending.

"Well it was too dark for me to explore, but the entrance is only a slit in a rock. Of what I could see inside in the dark it is quite large." Craig's voice had risen in excitement as he spoke.

"Would your uncle know of this cave, Craig?" I asked. "He is bound to know almost every nook and cranny around the loch."

"It is not near the loch, West! That's the point!"

I could almost imagine the boy's phone shaking with excitement at the other end. "Have you mentioned this to your uncle?"

"No.! He is in Fort William on business, and will not be back until tomorrow. I am on my own, except for Shep that is."

What sort of business would keep a man away overnight and leave a fifteen year old on his own? I thought.

"Don't worry, West, Uncle Ewen does this quite a lot when I'm here, it means he does not have to take Shep with him."

This time I heard the dog bark at the sound of his name.

"If I come up, do you think you could find this cave again?"

"Sure. Although it was dark by the time I got to the loch side I know where I came down off the hill."

"Good boy. I'll be at the house by 6am. Hope it's not too early for you?"

"Not when you're bringing Sue," Craig sounded a little embarrassed as he said this, as if disclosing his liking...love....lust for the girl.

"I don't think her bosses will give her the time off, even though it is to find her Gramps, " I said, and I heard the deep sigh of disappointment on the other end.

"OK" His voice had lost its excitement. "See you tomorrow

then."

"Ok,kid. And do me a favour, let's keep this between ourselves. Don't even let your uncle know should he phone to find out if you are all right."

After Craig had agreed and I had put the phone down, I glanced at my watch, it was a little past midnight. I knew that my snoring would have to wait, and even should I leave right away I would be up at Loch Arkaig long before 6 o'clock, but to go to bed now, I should only lie awake; better to be up and make myself ready for the journey. My only concern was that the boy had not exaggerated his discovery on the assumption that Sue would be coming with me. If he had, he would receive a high petrol bill, and a low kick where it hurt.

I left about half past one in the morning, complete with a flask of coffee and a few sandwiches I had made up from what I could find in the fridge.

At that time of the morning the roads were quiet and I made good time by- passing Stirling on the road to Doune, then on to Callander, which at that hour was completely deserted, in contrast to the day when I was last there with Sue at the beginning of my investigation into finding old Jock Fraser, now a little over two weeks past, and which now felt like a lifetime ago.

Taking advantage of the empty road I halted for a brief rest, and a sandwich or two, on a straight stretch of road which otherwise bent and twisted up the side of Loch Lubnaig.

Leaving my car I stood looking down at the loch, drinking in the cool fresh Highland air, attempting to focus my mind on the surrounding hills, and not what could be in store for me, (or the boy Craig) when the cave was found.

I did not stop again until I was on the Black Mount. Here, where most sightseers halt to absorb that vast panorama of mountains, I was the only one to marvel as I had always, at the beauty of Stob Ghabhar,Stob Coir'an, and Ben Tarav, with Loch Tulla below.

I gave a shudder in the morning's chill and got back into my car.

Rannoch Moor, lay a wild stretch of bog and lochan, this morning covered in a white shroud of mist. Bidean nam Bian, majestic in its halo of cloud, stood sentinel as it had done since the beginning of time in Glencoe. Soon I was crossing the bridge at Ballachulish and heading for Fort William.

The usually thriving tourist town was only beginning to come to life, as I arrived. Lorries hurrying to fill the supermarkets and shops: milk floats buzzing quietly along the streets delivering milk to hotel and guest house alike: the odd pedestrian or cyclist on their way to work to start another day.

A few minutes later I was at the Devil's Staircase and on the road to Loch Arkaig and Cour House, where I hoped Craig was not still asleep, now that Sue would not be with me.

I need not have worried. Shep came bounding to meet my car, desperate to know who this intruder was. I drew up the car and got out. Shep gave a growl and came slowly and cautiously towards me. "It's me," I said putting out a friendly hand and hoped I'd get it all back. "I'm not your breakfast." Shep didn't like my banter and gave a few angry barks, in reply. "That's terrible language for a wee dog," I chastised my canine adversary, "even if it is in the Gaelic."

"West!" The welcome voice of Craig reached me, and at the sound, the dog decided I must be a friend and wagged its tail as a signal, that I could now approach the house.

"I've put the kettle on. I thought you'd be here about this time." Craig, greeted me, though his eyes stared hopefully past me in the off chance that Sue might me in the car.

"Thanks, Craig, I could do with a cuppa."

Craig led me inside, leaving Shep to keep a watchful eye on me while he made the tea.

"Sue cannot come?" He handed me a mug of tea and a biscuit.

I took a sip and shook my head. "Too busy. Her bosses wouldn't give her the time off."

"Rotters," Craig said sourly.

"My thoughts exactly," I replied. "Now, where is this cave of yours?

"It's close to where we were before, when Sue fell into the loch at the sound of my uncle's gun. Do you remember?"

I nodded. "Let's go."

Sitting on the back seat of my car, Shep gave a whimper or two as he stared out of the window.

"I don't think Shep likes your driving very much, West," Craig chuckled.

"Well tell him in the Gaelic if he is not happy he can get out and walk," I answered light-heartedly, while watching a glimmer of sunlight appear on the other side of the loch.

At last Craig ordered me to stop. "This is the place, West, that's the rock where Sue fell into the water." He pointed through the windscreen.

We both got out with Shep immediately making for the nearest tree.

"I told you he didn't like your driving, West," Craig laughed.

"Hope he falls on his side," I muttered as the dog cocked its leg.

"I brought a torch." Craig took it out of the folds of his brown hooded jacket.

"So did I." I zipped up my jerkin against the nip in the air.

Ten minutes and a lot of puffing and panting later, as I laboured up the hillside, I halted to unzip that same garment, and regain my breath. "Old jock could not have made it up this climb at his age, Craig." I took out a hankie and wiped my brow. "I'm less than half his age and I'm knackered."

Craig turned to look down at me from where he stood a little way ahead, his face puzzled. "I thought it was the place where, Bonnie Prince Charlie's treasure is supposed to be hidden, that you were looking for?"

Now he had me. I knew within myself that old Jock Fraser was dead; having already deduced that he may well have been murdered when he had found the treasure, until the documents I had read in the safe had told me otherwise. Still, I wanted to find this cave just in the off chance it might be the one that I was searching for.

"We'll keep going." I let out a long sigh.

Suddenly the climb became less steep and here there was grass instead of scree or boulders to negotiate. Shep gave a growl and I watched him disappear into the trees.

"Up there!" Graig pointed to a rugged cluster of rocks. "The cave's up there!"

Perhaps the old man could have made the climb after all, providing that is, that this was the right cave.

I reached the rocks as Craig took off his hooded top. Underneath he wore the white T-shirt that he had loaned to Sue with the 'diesel' logo on it, although the 'D' and 'L' had been more prominent when Sue had worn it.

"It's only a slit in the rock, West, you will have to squeeze through it." Craig pointed to a rock where bushes almost hid the entrance.

"It was Shep who found it really, I took a look to see what he was sniffing around at. It was getting quite dark at that point, so I poked my torch in and managed to make out that it was quite deep inside. Uncle has never mentioned any cave here, so I don't think that it has been found before."

I discarded my jerkin, and the boy gave me an apologetic look, "I hope I haven't brought you all this way for nothing. But just think, West, if this is the right cave and the Prince's gold is inside we'll be rich and famous. The first to find it in over two hundred years," Craig's eyes lit up at the thought of what other secrets the cave might hold. "Unless that is that old Mr Fraser has not found it first."His voice had lost some of its excitement.

"We'll soon know, young Craig." I didn't want to curb the boy's enthusiasm.

I stepped to the slit and stuck my arm in, playing the torch around the interior as far as I could.

"Can't see much, but as you say it seems to be quite deep inside." I withdrew my arm and took a step back. "I'll squeeze through first, and hope my shirt doesn't catch. If I get stuck, it's up to you to pull me back out. OK?"

Craig gave me a grin. "OK fatty." The excitement had returned to his voice.

"Smart arse," I replied, grinning back.

A waist high spur of rock seemed to be the main obstacle, and manoeuvring round it was like going through a turnstile at a football match. Eventually I did so, and was surprised to find Craig by my side.

"Don't worry West, you could have done the same at my age. That's of course this cave was here before the ice age." I couldn't see him grin but I expected that he was.

"Another crack like that, and you won't see my age," I replied, playing my torch towards the centre of the cavern.

A few head high boulders stood in our way. I swept the ceiling to determine its height, then back to the boulders. The place was eerie to say the least, but not dank as I expected it to be. I shone my torch on the first boulder and rounded it, and heard Craig's deep breathing close to my ear.

From the first boulder to the far wall the floor appeared to be flat. I swung my torch to my right further up the interior, and almost dropped it at what lay there. Craig gripped my arm tight, and I heard him mutter something incoherently. Almost reluctantly I took a few steps closer. It was the right cave…the gold cave.

"That's not a body?" Craig's voice and torch shook as he shone it on the skeleton lying there.

"I'm afraid it is kid." I tried to sound the experienced crime fighter that I thought he would expect me to be. Little did he know, I was only a couple of knee shakes behind him.

"Is it old Mr Fraser?" Craig choked.

I drew closer shining my torch on what was left of what once had been a body. Only bones were left and a few pieces of rag. The shoes were the best preserved.

Craig had his torch beam on the grinning skull as if fascinated, but too afraid to move it away, the way one does when looking at something repulsive but always finding one's eyes drawn back to it.

"It's not the old man, Craig, this one has been here for a hell of a long time."

I explored the cave for a little while longer, then convinced there was nothing else to find, I gestured to the boy that we should leave.

Craig preceded me to the entrance and had just squeezed his way through when I heard him squeal and shout out my name. Regardless of the rocks scraping my skin as I rounded the 'turnstile' I found the boy fighting off a vicious attack by a Wildcat, it's claws tearing into his white T-shirt as it endeavoured to claw his face.

As quickly as I could I grabbed my jerkin off the ground where I had left it, and swung it at the animal, yelling and screaming at the top of my voice, while Craig had his hands up to shield his face. Suddenly the cat leaped down and into the cave leaving behind it two shaking individuals.

I lifted Craig's hooded top, and taking him by the arm led him a little way down the slope and away from the cave entrance.

"Let me see if you are all right." I took hold of his shoulders and peered into his frightened face. "No scratches there, Craig, you'll look as handsome as ever to the lassies."

He tried to smile, though in truth his body still shook from the day's double ordeal. Had I known what was in store I would not have let him come along. Then again had I known, would I myself have come along?

"Take off your top, and let me see what that bugger has done to you."

Giving him some help, Craig pulled the tattered garment over his head. I took it, or what was left of it, and studying it I said, "You'll not be lending this to Sue again, I think."

"No." Craig, stared at the top, and I knew what was going through his mind, that this was his only memento of the girl he admired.

I took out my hankie and wiped the blood from where the cat had scratched his chest. He lifted his arm and I cleaned the blood off from just under his arm pit.

I stepped back. "There, that's the best I can do for you just now young man. Best that I get you back home."

Craig nodded and I held out his hooded top to him.

"What the hell have you done to him?" I heard the yell, Shep barking and snarling at my feet.

I swung round, Ewen Cameron ran at me, shotgun swinging. I managed to duck under the first intended blow, and I heard Craig shout out to his uncle to stop, but whatever had incensed the man it was not going to stop him. I hit the big man midriff with my head knocking him on to the grass banking, the gun flying from his grasp. He took the blow and in seconds was clawing at the grass for his weapon. I kicked it aside, and stood back in the hope of explaining what had happened. He lunged at me and succeeded in grabbing one of my legs and I went down, twisting quickly to get on top of him, and for a moment I considered pulling his beard. "Will you listen!" I bellowed at him but he came at me again. He was bigger and stronger than me:so much for city living I thought, or country dying, such as now. What was worse, Shep also decided to join in, growling and tugging at my trouser leg.

It was Craig who finally came to my rescue by attempting to pull his uncle off me, and shouting that I had not harmed him, and that it was a Wildcat who had done this to him.

At last Ewen seemed to realise what the boy was saying and let go of me before he killed me..well a few punches short of it. He got up and stood back watching me rise shakily to my feet.

"What's the boy trying to say?" Ewen's heavy breathing matched my own as he asked the question, and in turn looked at Craig for some sort of an explanation.

I pulled my trouser leg down where Shep had tried to make it into a pair of shorts.

"It was a Wildcat who did this to the boy." I didn't feel like being too cordial to the man who had tried to half kill me. "Craig found the cave. It's up there." I nodded in that direction.

Ewen looked at his nephew for confirmation. "When did you find it, laddie?"

"He phoned me last night when you were in Fort William," I said. "I told him not to bother telling you until I came up here and saw for myself, whether it was the right cave or not."

I saw the relief spread over Craig's face at my explanation, and I hoped it would prevent the man asking the boy any other awkward questions about not telling him about the cave.

"There's a body inside, Uncle Ewen." The boy tried to soften the situation between his uncle and me. "West says it's not old Mr Fraser, as it has been in there too long."

Ewen gave me a look asking me if what his nephew had said was true.

"The boy's right. It's only a skeleton. It has been there for many a long year. Long before old Jock Fraser went missing."

"And if not old Jock, who?" he asked in a tone to disguise his embarrassment at having jumped to the wrong conclusion at my attacking his nephew.

Now in the cold light of reasoning he must have realised that I would have had to be a big lassie to have attacked Craig by scratching him. And even so, to what purpose?

"I think I know who." I stared at him, and although I had not forgiven him for trying to beat me up, I needed his help. "Can you give me a couple of days before you report this to the police?" I asked as civilly as I could.

"Can't you tell me a wee bit more about all this?"

I shook my head. "I would rather not at this stage, just on the off chance I may be wrong," again , I said under my breath.

The gamekeeper stooped and picked up his gun, and I carefully kept my eyes on him.

"We best get you back, laddie, and have those scratches looked at." He threw me a look. "A Wildcat you say? Aye, that's what the wee dog was on about, was it. It was him that led me here. I am just not long back from the town, and read your wee note. Craig, that you would be around here somewhere, though you never mentioned a cave."

Instantly I knew the boy would be in trouble if he could not offer a valid explanation.

"As I have said, I asked him not to....just in case it turned out to be nothing at all."

"Or that I had killed old Jock for having found the Bonnie Prince's treasure. Eh Barns?"

"No, Ewen, I already knew you hadn't. It is something else much more sinister. I am sorry if I used Craig, but I needed him to show me the cave, you will understand."

The big man nodded. "Aye. Now let's get the laddie cleaned up." He pointed at my dishevelled appearance and gave me an apologetic smile, "as well as yourself."

He took a couple of steps away, and said, over his shoulder, "I will have a look inside yon cave tomorrow."

After a mug of tea and a mountain of sandwiches, I said my goodbyes at Cour House a little past one o'clock. Craig had brightened up a bit after his morning's ordeal, and I gave him a Twenty Pound note to buy a new T-shirt, and a little extra for his time, which to give the boy his due he was reluctant to take. I also suggested he visit the hospital to have his injuries attended to as well as a tetanus jag, to which he turned up his nose and said he would be all right. I left it at that. I probably would have acted the same at his age.

The mountains and lochs that had never ceased to fill me with pride, and that this was my land..my country, for the first time held no pleasure for me, now I saw them as nothing more than a mere obstruction to my journey home.

By the time I reached North Berwick, I was dead tired and wanted first to go home, have a shower, and change of clothes; instead I made for my office.

The sound of laughter floating up the corridor as I turned the key in the lock seemed to sooth the turmoil in my head, and also the thought of what was to come and what I must do, should my deductions prove correct.

I stooped and picked up the usual junk mail and sorted out my bills. I sank down at my desk and swivelled the chair round to face the window, and the sight of the beach with the Bass Rock in the distance. Here at last was sanctuary, and I felt a comfort at being back amongst normal people doing normal things. I allowed myself a wee smile. I'd go down, say hello to Maggie, and cadge a cup of coffee, although it was her and the office girls company that I really sought. Then just as I had finally decided on doing so, the phone rang, it was my brother Fenton.

"Hello, West," my perpetually cheerful brother greeted me. "Don't you ever switch on your mobile? I have been trying to reach you all day; put me in a spot you have."

"How come?" I asked wrinkling my brows.

"Well, I've been stalling until I found you. We've found the car."

I knew instantly who, and what he meant, but just the same I had to ask, "Old jock Fraser?"

"The same. Got his name from his car registration number. The old guy's dead of course; has been for quite some time."

"Heart attack?" I asked hopefully.

"Only if brought on by a heavy blow, and he fell in the bog."

To say I was shocked was an understatement. I swallowed and asked as I gazed unseeing out of the window. "Where did you find the car?"

" Near Dunbeg, on the road to Oban."

"Christ," I swore. "No wonder we didn't find it. What was it doing away down there?"

"No idea buddy. Seems the old guy owns a whisky Company down your way. Maybe we can find that out when we ask those in his Company. The crime is in my jurisdiction, so it will be up to me to handle the case. Of course Fettes will have to tell his next of kin should the old man have any."

"He hasn't. Do me a favour Fenton, let me try something first, and I guarantee I will have your killer before you can say, promotion."

There was silence at the other end until I heard him say, as having given it his most serious consideration, "Why? How can you do that?"

It was then I told him of my suspicions.

CHAPTER FOUR

After Fenton's news I phoned the distillery. It was Sue who answered, and I tried to sound cheerful, by asking how her day was. After she had given me her woes and a few unladylike words relating to her employers, I got round to my reason for calling.

"Sue, do you think you could arrange for me to meet your employers tonight at old Jock's house? Say about eight o'clock, there are a few unanswered questions I should like to ask them."

"It will have to be important; we are still trying to catch up after the fire."

"It is," I assured her. I did not want to tell her about Gramps at this stage.

"Ok. I'll phone you on your mobile if it does not suit them."

It better suit, I thought. Out loud I said, "Good… Oh, and Sue, make sure Neil Grant is there as well."

My thoughts of coffee had disappeared, and I decided to make for home and have that shower and change of clothes I promised myself. Food was out of the question, as my stomach was in knots with the thought of what I was about to do.

Earlier that evening as I was about to leave, Amanda MacDonald suggested; or to be precise, 'demanded' that I meet at her house instead of old Jock's, and gave me directions on how to get there.

It was Amanda herself who let me in. "I am sorry to inconvenience you, Mr West, but I believe there might have been a break-in at old Jock's house. The police are still investigating."

Damn, I thought, Harry and I had been most careful. "Did they get anything," I asked and tried to sound concerned.

"Went for the safe," Simon answered as I sat down in a room that put old Jock's to shame by its sheer opulence.

"I told the old man to have it updated, but he wouldn't listen; held on to that key like grim death," Neil informed me, and I wished he had not used that terminology.

"What's so important that it cannot wait until tomorrow at the office?" Simon gave an artificial yawn, to remind me of just how hard he worked at the distillery.

I cleared my throat and shot Sue a furtive glance, before answering the man. I could well understand her unease at being here, it could not be easy having to tolerate these people, after work, and at this time of night. She stared at me, and drew her legs under her chair, waiting for me to start.

"Now that you have informed Detective Constable Thomson that old Jock is missing, I took it upon myself to inform my brother Fenton who has been seconded to the Force up in Inverness, about the possibility of the old man being up there. Upon this information from Detective Thomson and myself, my brother and Northern Constabulary have been searching for old Jock and his car. So far without success," I lied.

"Therefore, since Mr Fraser did not find his way here to attend the promotion, we can safely say something has happened to him." I shot Sue a glance to see how she was taking it. She had taken out a hankie and dabbed at an eye.

"My brother also informed me as they have exhausted all the likely and unlikely places around Loch Arkaig area and down to Glencoe, and Rannoch Moor, that they will now extend their search as far south as Oban, on the off chance he may have started for home by that route instead of Glencoe.

"Should anything have happened to the old boy, say unnaturally," Neil asked, "what then? If he has been dead for…"

"Stop it! Stop it!" Sue was on her feet, her hankie at her eyes. "I don't want to hear anymore."

"If anything has happened to Mr Fraser, forensics will soon find out. If he has been robbed while in his car, it is most likely that whoever did it will leave some evidence behind; and DNA for instance will find the most minute drop of blood or hair."

"That makes me chief suspect," Sue sobbed. "I've been in Gramps car more times that I can mention."

"Not really. Forensics will eliminate your DNA in places where they would expect to find them. So you need not worry Sue."

"What's your honest opinion, Mr West? Assuming that the Old Man is dead, that is." Amanda asked.

I watched Sue sink back down in her chair, I would not have been at all surprised had she left, but she didn't.

" Should Mr Fraser not have died from natural causes, but instead, murdered." It was the first time that word had been used and I saw heads jerk up in my direction, "there must have been two attackers,"

"Why?" Neil challenged.

"Say for example the old man was attacked in his car, either when he drew up in a lay-by to rest, or whether it was up some side road, there must have been another car to take them away."

"Or they left him where they killed him and drove off in his car." Neil suggested.

I nodded in agreement. "Or his attacker could already have been in the car, a hitchhiker, or someone he knew, but since his car has not been found I would put my money, on finding Mr Fraser in his car."

"In the direction of Oban?" Simon sipped a whisky. He had not entered into the conversations of assumptions.

"I should think so, now that every other feasible place has been searched."

"I think you're wrong Barns. I bet when the old bugger's found that he died of a heart attack, either from too much floosie," he chortled at his own humour, "or it was those damned hills, he and my grandfather never stopped climbing." Simon reached for his drink on the table beside him. "All for what? Searching for some bloody treasure that no longer exists?"

"If old Fraser has been murdered, I hope they get whoever did it." Amanda let out a little breath.

"Oh, they will," I assured her. "Forensic will see to that, unless that is, whoever is or are responsible have not set fire to the car. Then that will make it more difficult."

"What happens now, Mr Barns?" Neil asked.

"Now that the police have been notified of Mr Fraser's disappearance, they will call and take statements to establish where you all were at certain times , should the old man be dead, that is, and has died in suspicious circumstances. They will also ask someone to identify the body."

"Bloody hell!" Simon leapt to his feet. "Now we're all bloody suspects!" He walked quickly to the drinks cabinet and poured himself another whisky without offering one to anyone.

"Well at least I know I was in York." Sue screwed up her nose. "At least I think I was, when Gramps was… I suppose it depends when it happened."

Simon sat back down, his temper still flailing. "As if we hadn't enough to contend with without the police sniffing around since that German guy got himself murdered in Edinburgh; all because they found one of our business cards on him."

I stood up. "However, there is still a slim chance that Mr Fraser is still alive," I lied, and watched for their reaction.

As I started for the door, Amanda made to show me out. "Thank you for calling, Mr Barns, we appreciate it. I am sure they will find old Jock, and let's hope he is alive and well."

On previous ocassions the road to the Highlands via Fort William never failed to excite me, with its mountains and lochs, now it was nothing more than a black strip of bitumen taking me to where I least wanted to be. This time the only difference to my journey was my taking the A85 at Tyndrum and heading towards Oban.

The Pass of Brander was eerie still at that time of night, and only a couple of lights shone in Taynuilt as I sped through, and on to Connel where I was to meet Fenton.

I had left straight after telling the MacDonalds, Neil Grant and Sue of what I had thought might have happened to the old guy. It was the end of the saga.

Fenton was waiting for me at Connel as arranged. "Leave your car here, West." He introduced me to two police officers and we got in his car.

"We found the car near Dunbeg," one of the officers said as way of starting the conversation.

"Why the hell away out here?" the second one asked. "The old boy was supposed to be treasure hunting away up at Loch Arkaig?" Evidently West had not briefed them on the 'why' but only the 'where' and what other details he thought necessary, should my theory prove to be wrong.

At last we reached Dunbeg

"We'll leave the car hidden here." Fenton pointed back the way we had come, to a dirt road away to our left. "The car was found up there."

I nodded and followed the officers of the law as they started off in that direction.

After about a hundred yards or so we walked up what could only be described as a track, where we were halted by a uniformed figure emerging out of the bushes.

"Everything is in place, sir," the constable addressed my brother.

"Good, Anderson. Now the only thing we can do is wait."

More than a half hour had passed before we heard the sound of a car changing gears and entering the track. A few feet away from where I stood hidden, it stopped and the door opened. The shadowy figure got out and walked to the boot, opened it and took out a petrol can and walked to where Fenton had told me they had found the car, switched on the torch, and played it on the bog beyond.

I heard a sharp intake of breath even from where I emerged from the bushes. "It's not there, Sue," I said. "The car's not there."

Fenton let me talk to Sue after her confession. She was sitting looking at the table, a forlorn pitiful figure as I entered the room.

"Why, Sue?" I asked as I sat down across the table from her.

"Why?" She looked up defiantly at me. "I'll tell you why. If you had an opportunity not to have to work for those... I hate them all..those snobs.." Anger showed on every inch of her face. A face I no longer knew. At first when I saw her sitting there, I had felt sorry for her, now she showed not even the slightest hint of remorse. This was not the girl I had come to love...well at least hold some affection for.

As she looked at me, her features softened slightly. "When did you first know, West?"

"After I had the safe opened. Even then I was not completely sure. Deep down I hoped it was not you."

She managed a little smile. "You mean you and me?"

I nodded. "Why not? It could have worked."

"Poor West, you could never have given me what old Gramps could have."

"You mean the Will? That's what made you do it, wasn't it?"

She shrugged. "Do you know the full story?"

"I think I know most of it. However, I should have picked up the signs earlier."

"Such as?" she asked.

"That day you fell outside the hotel in Fort William, and I took you to the chemist and I saw the midge bites on your arm. You said you had just come back from York, so unless there were some Scottish midgies down there on holiday, you must have been up that way before."

"Clever you."

"Not really. Because it was you, I gave you the benefit of the doubt. Then there was that little fiasco of you being shot and falling into the water. All because young Craig was getting too close to discovering the cave...the cave you had previously visited with old Gramps and he told you about Archie's confession. That little stunt had me also thinking Ewen Cameron had something to do with Gramps disappearance. It worked, it took me off the scent.

But it was the safe that lent itself to more clues. In it were Gramp's wallet, watch and mobile. So whoever had done the deed must also have the old man's safe key, and if so, was the only one who could have sent those fake text messages.

Old gramps had told you that you would benefit from his estate, and when I read this it made all the difference to my theory. Before I had done so, I saw no reason why you should wish the old man dead. On the contrary with him gone you would most likely be out of a job; that's if Simon got his way, which he would, now that he would become sole owner of the Company."

"You are one smart cookie, Mr West Barns. You will go a long way in your chosen profession."

I was aware of myself blushing, but not at the intended compliment. "Almost as smart as you Sue. Why did you leave those things in the safe? I could very well understand you leaving the Will there, but why the other items?"

"Oh they are gone, now. I got shot of the mobile, and wallet...must have been after your little safecracking job?" she laughed.

"And the confession?"

"That I safely tucked away, should 'cold eyes,' she looked at me and laughed, "refuse to accept me as an equal partner."

"So tell me the rest, Sue. How did it all begin?"

Sue sighed and sat back in her chair. "I was on my way back from York when Gramps texted me. That's when he said he had found it. Naturally I thought he meant Prince Charlie's gold from the '45 Rebellion. I told him I was on my way and that I would meet him in the car park in Fort William at noon the next day.

"So when you put on your little act that first time I met you at old Jock's house and you pretended that you had just arrived from York, you had in fact already met the old man in Fort William." I clicked my teeth. "I should have checked that out."

Sue gave me a sheepish grin. "Not bad acting I must say."

"Oh I grant you that Sue. All that sobbing and worry over the old man, and you knowing all along what had happened to him. You must have had a good laugh at all of us, especially me."

She bit her lip. "Not all of it was acting, West. My tears were genuine enough...tears of remorse for what I had done to an old man who had helped me, but, who would have taken away my one and only chance of a great and secure future, should he have been free to tell what he knew."

"And me?" I asked.

"Had we met under different circumstances, it might have worked between us." She splayed her hands in a gesture of surrender. "As it is..?"

She went on, "Anyhow, as I was saying, Gramps was very distraught when I met him: not the Gramps I knew. He asked me to take him to the loch in my car and hopefully slip past Ewen Cameron, should that man be about. We were lucky, although Ewen did see us, he did not recognise my car.

Gramps asked me to stop at the place that I had my little accident," she smiled wanly at me, "then we started the climb to the cave, and I was glad I had kept my climbing boots in my car. It took the old man quite a time to get there, although I must say I was none too fresh myself. Gramps explained that he and Archie had found this cave a few years before the War, and as there had been nothing in it of interest, he for one had never had any reason to go back, except two days before I arranged to meet him. Now he had to see for himself if what Archie MacDonald had written in his confession was true. He took me there so that I too, would know the truth."

I watched Sue twist her handkerchief around her fingers, knowing what she must have felt when she entered that dismal place.

"Gramps stood back and shone his torch in to the centre and I almost dropped dead with shock."

"You saw the skeleton."

Sue nodded. "It was then Gramps told me what his old friend Archie had written in his confession."

It had all begun in the late nineteen thirties. Old Archie...or young Archie as he was then, loved climbing in the Alps: that's where later he sustained an injury that was to keep him out of the War. He also loved everything German, and at first, admired Hitler for the way he had eradicated his country's unemployment.

Amongst other things, Archie also hated Communism, so when

Germany went to war against Russia, he saw Hitler as a saviour; the right man to lead Europe against what he saw as evil. His only disappointment was that Britain was at war with Germany and not on their side against bolshevism.

Gramps went on to tell me, that Archie was not the only man to hold such views, that there many other sympathisers in Britain who thought similarly. Now came Archie's chance. If Britain could be brought to the negotiating table, it would leave Hitler to deal fully with the Russians.

"Have you forgotten, Sue, that I have also read old Archie's confession, albeit after you did?"

"So you know, Archie decided that the best way he could neutralise this country was to assist in the Nazi plot to swamp her economically, with forged British banknotes,"

"And gold," I said. "Don't forget the gold."

"How could, I?" Sue sighed.

"Archie decided to help by arranging for the Nazis to land gold bullion on the shores of Loch Nevis, and have it transported to the cave he and Gramps had discovered. Gramps knew nothing of this of course, as he was away fighting abroad at this time..North Africa I believe.

"Of course Archie knew what he was doing was High Treason, but he firmly believed that he was doing it for the best. However, he needed someone to melt down the bars as he could not hope to dispose of them with…"

"A dirty great swastika on them," I suggested.

"Precisely." Sue halted, and tears came to her eyes.

I decided to help her. "So Gramps told you the man Archie had help him was your own grandfather."

Sue nodded and burst into tears. "Gramps pointed to the skeleton. 'That is your grandfather, Sue, he said." Sue choked back a sob. "Gramps said that Archie's confession said he had killed him because my grandfather had wanted more money for doing the melting down of the gold, or he would go to the police. West, I could not believe that I was looking at what remained of my grandfather. All those years my grandmother and my mother not ever knowing what had happened to him, and all the while he was there, lying in that cave."

I took over. "When Archie got to know what the Nazis were

really doing in Russia and Europe …and especially to those in concentration camps, he decided against using the gold for its original purpose. But now he was in a dilemma; if he were to tell the authorities he must surely be imprisoned, or even worse, so he did the next best thing, he used it to build up his own business. Which he did very successfully, making Jock Fraser an equal partner, probably to save his own conscience, and what Jock had been through, fighting against a man who at first he had seen as a hero. But later, according to his confession, he had finally learned what Hitler and his regime were really like."

"That's what really killed Gramps. He could not reconcile that he himself had prospered from, 'blood money' he called it that day in the cave," Sue sobbed.

"Then what happened Sue?"

"Gramps said somehow he would pay all the money back to the rightful owners, those who had lost everything during the War. How he proposed to do that I don't know, and I told him so. It was then he told me I would still be provided for: become a full partner after he was gone. He would also compensate my mother and grandmother, for my grandfather's death. It was the first I knew he had left me anything in his Will, or what he had intended."

"How come you both finished up on the road to Oban?" I asked wrinkling my brows.

"I suggested that we head for Oban, spend the night there and talk things over in the morning. I drove him back to Fort William where Gramps picked up his car and he followed me. On the way there I could not believe what had happened, suddenly I realised I would inherit the fortune which Gramps was going to throw away. It was then I decided to try and get him to change his mind. As luck would have it he signalled to me that he wanted to stop. He passed me and drove up a dirt road. I left my car on the main road and waited for him to return. At first I thought he had wanted to relieve himself, then, as he had not come back, I got out and walked up the path. He was standing there looking across the moor, crying softly to himself. He saw me and said, 'Sue all those men, women and children all gassed and put into ovens, and I have used their money to make myself rich; worse still, that my partner should have been a willing accomplice in this. It doesn't bear thinking about, Sue.'

"I tried to console him, but it was no good. I gave him all the reasons I could think of not only to make him feel better within himself, but also to think of the shame it would bring upon my own family. He would have none of it.

It was as I stood there that I became suddenly angry at this old man - to me he was a selfish old man. He had given me with one hand and was about to take it away with the other. Oh, I know I was to be left something, and I would be a great deal better off than I had ever been. But it was the chance of being an equal partner in the Company instead of a secretary kept under sufferance by Simon MacDonald, and patronised or tolerated by Neil and Amanda that I was going to lose, that angered me most."

As I listened I understood how she must have felt. Jock Fraser was going to hand over his millions to whom? The rightful owners of the gold were long since dead. Who were their surviving relatives? All Sue knew was, that Simon would come out of it best, his money would remain intact, unless she decided to blackmail him. But at that stage she still had not actually seen Archie's written confession. Therefore, to her way of thinking, it should be |Simon who should pay the compensation, not old Jock, but there was little chance of him doing that. No matter who was to blame, the Company would suffer should it hit the Press, and this is what would happen once it was known that old Jock was giving away his millions.

Now came the worse part I thought as I looked at the girl across the table.

Sue must have known what was in my mind for she started. "All I could think of was losing the money, what my folks had suffered, and my grandfather, and what would happen to me? All I knew was, here was an old man, who had very little left to lose by giving away most of his wealth, whereas I had my whole life in front of me, and although he had told me I was beneficiary in his Will, I did not know how much would be left should he carry out his intention of compensation."

Sue stopped and looked at me. "As Gramps stood staring across the moor, I lifted a stone and hit him on the back of the head. He went down without as much as a moan, and I hit him again." She stopped for a moment, swallowed and went on. "I took everything off him in the odd chance that when he was found it might go down as a mugging that had gone wrong. Then I managed to roll him into the bog."

    Sue stared me in the eye. "Somehow, at the time I felt no remorse, only anger, as I watched him disappear beneath that peat water. The rest you know," she said with a sigh.

Epilogue

"You'll be heading back home, now that it is all over, West?" Fenton said as I met him in his office."

"Suppose so," I answered dismally.

"Don't know why you're down. You've solved your first murder case since leaving the Force, besides helping that eejit Thomson to lock away those arsonists that tried to burn down your clients' distillery. It can do nothing but good for your business; all in just two weeks or so." Fenton gave a hearty laugh. "Who knows, given another day or so, you might have put Simonson away too for us."

I shuddered at the name.

Fenton grew serious, and his voice changed as he said softly. "You liked her, didn't you brother?"

I nodded.

"It was you planting the idea that the only way to destroy D.N.A. was to burn the car, that had the lassie driving to the spot, otherwise it might have taken longer to nail her. Even had she said she had nothing to do with the old man's death but had decided to follow you as she had a feeling that you had lied and did in fact know that the car had already been found, there was no way she could explain how she followed you when you had left your car at Connel. Of course the clincher was her standing there with a can of petrol in her hand. Run out of petrol and was walking to a service station via a couple of bogs? I think not, West," Fenton chuckled. But I was in no mood to share in his witticisms.

It had been an even longer drive from where I had left my brother in Inverness. I scarcely saw the scenery for my mind was still on Sue, and what would happen to her, and I didn't relish the idea of testifying against her in court.

By the time I reached North Berwick and home I was 'knackered' as they say in China. Well, Outer Mongolia really…Inner Mongolians don't get out much, so I drove to my flat for a well earned rest.

It was the next day that I heard from Amanda MacDonald, asking me to come to the distillery and pick up my well earned cheque (my words, not hers). She was sitting at her husband's desk when I got there.

"You got back I see. Quite a long journey from Inverness."

"You know?"

"Yes, your brother phoned me. The bitch has asked for a solicitor," she seethed.

I tried to control my anger; I'd say nothing until I had my cheque in my red hot hand, and then some.

Amanda slid the cheque across the desk. It was not done in a malicious way, more of 'will this trifling amount suit you?' as she looked up at me with a self satisfied mocking look.

I took a look at the cheque, it was not only a few hundred more than I had expected but a thousand. I could pay my bills, eat and look for old Mrs MacKenzie's dog.

"Very generous," I said as I slid it into my pocket. "Then again you can afford to be, Mrs MacDonald, now that Sue and your husband are out of the way."

For the first time I saw her blush as my inference hit the mark.

"What do you mean by that remark, Mr Barns?" she asked angrily.

"You know that your husband, believing old Mr MacDonald to be dead, did a deal with Millar Mackay to sell him the Company as he believed himself to be sole owner. Of course he did not know that old Jock had left his half of the Company to Sue, or he might have thought differently. Anyhow, unknown to Mackay, his partner Jack Grey had the idea that should your distillery suddenly go up in flames, he could purchase the Company for much less."

Amanda's eyes opened wide in astonishment. "The dirty."

"Who, Grey or your husband?" I allowed myself a chuckle.

"Both," she stormed.

"So as your husband and Sue have been arrested for murder, and will probably be convicted, and if so cannot benefit from the estate, you are the happy sole owner of the Company."

I casually leaned against the wall and watched the hate boil at the thought that I was in possession of all the facts. So to turn the screw a little tighter I went on.

"As you know Simon has been arrested for the murder of the German gentleman. Quite an unfortunate coincidence wasn't it that the poor bloke should arrive on the day of the promotion."

"You know the story?" Amanda asked.

"Don't you?" I said a little surprised.

"Not all of it."

Briefly I related the story of old Archie's treachery, of which to be honest she knew nothing, as had Simon, until the German arrived.

Seemingly one of the German soldier's who had helped to carry the bullion from the submarine to the cave, heard the name MacDonald mentioned; not that it was of any significance to him at the time. Soon after however, the poor bloke was transferred to the dreaded Eastern Front, where he was captured and held in a Russian Gulag until the mid fifties, to return a broken man. He had either forgotten about his little excursions to Loch Nevis, or had cast them aside, which was reasonable enough considering what else he must have gone through. Then just before he died when relating some of his war experiences to his son, he mentioned old Archie's name and what he had been doing there in Scotland. At the time his son had thought nothing of it until an article had appeared in a newspaper telling of a book 'The Red Book' that had been published, listing British Nazi sympathisers during the War, who were members calling themselves 'The Right Club', some of whom were in the Government of the day, or M.Ps. or titled aristocrats, and it was there that he saw old Archie's name.

Believing he had stumbled onto a fortune, he had informed a newspaper reporter, who had taken up the search.

"The one who called here to see, Simon?" Amanda interrupted.

"The one and the same."

"Simon confessed, you know." Amanda looked up at me standing there.

"To you," I asked.

She shook her head. "To the police. Seemingly, Simon had gone to this reporter guy's hotel in Edinburgh with the intention of paying him off, for he knew that although the War was many years past, that many of our clients would not be so ready to forgive and forget, especially those who had suffered at the hands of the Nazis, especially the Jews. Whatever Simon had offered him was not enough. The story was too big." Amanda sighed. "I don't really know what happened, but what I do know, is that my husband did not go there with the intention of killing that man."

"But he did," I said. "And somehow I believe that you are not completely devastated by the consequences." Hold on West, I thought, you should wait until the cheque is cleared before you annoy this one.

Amanda MacDonald's face turned an angry red, one to match her temper. She rose, but before she could vent her spleen upon me, she was interrupted.

"Amanda darling, what are we going to do..?"

Neil Grant stood there open mouthed, he had not known I was there.

In turn I gave each a smile. "So now I know who gave me that nasty bump on my head, yon night that I inadvertently interrupted,... something?"

Later, as I stood looking out of my office window, it was raining heavily, hiding the Bass Rock under a grey cloud. In the street below, people, umbrellas aloft were walking their dogs, each no doubt wishing they had bought a goldfish instead.

It was as I was about to turn away that I saw the wee white dog sitting there, looking up at me, offering me a paw.

"So you have come to give yourself up have you, you wee mutt?" I shouted at the window, then I was out of the door and running down the corridor, determined to close my third and final case to date.

The End

Author's Note

Although this novella is a work of fiction, the Red Book which contains the names of those who were members of the Right Club sympathetic to the Nazi cause, does exist.

Printed in Great Britain
by Amazon